Trafika Europe

Edited by Andrew Singer

Essential

New European

Literature

VOL. 1

The Pennsylvania State University Press

University Park, Pennsylvania

Library of Congress Cataloging-in-Publication Data

Names: Singer, Andrew, editor.
Title: Trafika Europe : essential new
    European literature / edited by Andrew
    Singer.
Description: University Park, Pennsylvania
    : The Pennsylvania State University
    Press, [2016]–
Summary: "A collection of fiction and poetry
    representing the literature of cultures
    across Europe, including Shetland
    Scots, Occitan, Latvian, Polish,
    Armenian, Italian, Hungarian, German,
    Slovenian, Faroese and Icelandic"—
    Provided by publisher.
Identifiers: LCCN 2015050953 | ISBN
    9780271074658 (pbk. : alk. paper)
Subjects: LCSH: European literature—21st
    century. | European fiction—21st
    century. | European poetry—21st
    century.
Classification: LCC PN6014 .T68 2016 | DDC
    8098.8/994—dc23
LC record available at http://lccn.loc.
    gov/2015050953

Published by
The Pennsylvania State University Press,
University Park, PA 16802–1003

The Pennsylvania State University Press is
a member of the Association of American
University Presses.

It is the policy of The Pennsylvania State
University Press to use acid-free paper.
Publications on uncoated stock satisfy
the minimum requirements of American
National Standard for Information
Sciences—Permanence of Paper for Printed
Library Material, ANSI Z39.48–1992.

Typeset by Regina Starace
Printed and bound by Sheridan Books
Composed in Freight Text Pro
Printed on 50# Natures Natural

contents

editor's welcome

Europe is vast, and vastly changing. Culturally, Europe is understood as the quilt of overlapping people and nations all the way from the Atlantic Ocean to the Caspian Sea. The continent is home to three-quarters of a billion people, with more than 225 living native languages; some forty-seven countries make up the Council of Europe. And for the first time in history—just now, in this generation—a majority of people from a majority of all these places in Europe have one single common shared auxiliary language: English.

So *Trafika Europe* is starting out on a grand adventure to explore this cultural richness and to share the results of this journey with our English-language readers—not just native English speakers but also those who share this journal across the continent and beyond. Our hope is to contribute to a larger conversation about European identity, help this conversation continue to grow in open and mutual regard, and attract new readers to some amazing work going on in European literature today.

The modest selections in this volume pull together some of the very best of our very best—bringing focused highlights of contemporary European literature culled from our first four quarterly journal issues. The fourteen chapters each feature a different author. We've got seven works of fiction and seven selections of poems—from seven women and seven men, from cultures spanning the continent: new writing translated from Shetland Scots and Occitan, Latvian and Polish, Armenian, Italian, Hungarian, German, and Slovenian, Faroese, and Icelandic. These pieces range from expansive and Old World to intellectual and avant-garde, from highly narrative to a little mystical. We've got a long way to go yet on our journey—and we're so pleased to share with you along the way *Essential*

New European Literature, volume 1. It's a selection of pieces that have really stood out for us over our first year.

We begin with a chapter from *A Treatise on Shelling Beans*, by Wiesław Myśliwski, one of eastern Europe's grand novelists. In wry, gentle, piqued prose, the old caretaker of a holiday housing complex in rural Poland regales a stranger with tales from his life and so from the life of Poland past. Another highlight, from the tiny culture of the Faroe Islands, is a healthy excerpt from Jóanes Nielsen's *The Brahmadells: A North Atlantic Chronicle.* This is the first work from Faroese ever to receive a major international publishing contract and thus the most important news of Faroese literature in English in our times. To celebrate its English debut in our pages, we're showcasing a hefty chapter here.

There is taut, evocative prose from Jón Kalman Stefánsson's *The Heart of Man*, the final novel of his masterful Icelandic trilogy. And there's poetry from Shetland Scots, a dialect that retains strong ties to Old Norse, with echoes in the musculature of present-day English. Christine De Luca, the poet laureate of Edinburgh, was surprised that we're presenting these poems of hers only in English "translation." You'll be able to hear her reading her original versions in Shetland dialect at our site.

There's sensual and profound poetry by Latvian poet Edvīns Raups. We're also thrilled to include the first novel by a leading Latvian poet, playwright, and intellectual, Māra Zālīte—an autobiographical memoir of life on her grandfather's farm after her family's return from Siberia.

Then there's dreamlike prose from Slovenian master novelist Marko Sosič and perfect poetry—in pieces like supernally polished stones—from native French-Occitan poet Aurélia Lassaque. This is countered by stunning, postapolcalyptic verse—mapping the rigors of the body onto the *mortis* of society, perhaps—from Italian poet Vincenzo Bagnoli.

Another great highlight is a "wreath" of fifteen sonnets by Hungarian-Roma poet László Sárközi. Mentored by the now deceased enfant terrible of Hungarian literature, György Faludy, Sárközi explores the strained relation between his Roma and Hungarian identity in this candid, hard, beautiful sonnet sequence.

Farther east, you'll find new Armenian fiction by Nara Vardanyan. And check out the dense, incantatory litany of longing by Ewa Chrusciel, in English-speaking verse peizing a Poland she's left behind. You can find an animated video we've made of one of these poems, "Prayer," on our *Trafika Europe* YouTube page.

There's superb new fiction by Stefanie Kremser, who is representative of a new kind of European: raised in Brazil, studied in Germany, and now living with her Catalan husband in Barcelona. Finally, Scottish nature poet Mandy Haggith shares tree poems, each inspired by the essence of a different tree from the old Gaelic tree alphabet.

We've included long, generous selections from some of Europe's finest living novelists and poets—rounded out with sumptuous photos of Europe by master photographer Mark Chester. As the European experiment and identity continue to evolve, this sort of cultural window can give surprising insight into where we've been and where we are today. As for where we're going, well, that's up to us.

Please check back with us often as we continue this exciting journey— and thanks.

Andrew Singer / Director, *Trafika Europe*
Some of the best new literature from Europe
trafikaeurope.org
twitter.com/TrafikaEurope
facebook.com/TrafikaEurope

A Treatise on Shelling Beans

(novel excerpt)

WIESŁAW MYŚLIWSKI

Born in the village of Dwikozy, Poland, in 1932, Wiesław Myśliwski straddles worlds—he is just old enough to remember older ways yet born into a wartime that defies understanding. His works mix a relentless, sweetly resigned nostalgia with an exquisite palette of storytelling tools, for a sustained, flowing narrative that is engagingly likeable, despite his characters' tragic flaws of birth, happenstance, culture, and inclination.

This is a style best engaged in depth, so we're presenting a generous sample—a whole chapter—from his recently translated novel, *A Treatise on Shelling Beans*. The book is told by a caretaker at a holiday housing complex, who is met by a stranger seeking beans; this sets the caretaker off on a long, weaving recounting of his phases of life experience and the Polish history he's lived through along the way. The *Times Literary Supplement* calls this work a "marvel of narrative seduction, a rare double masterpiece of storytelling and translation."

Translated from Polish by Bill Johnston.

You didn't know him? That's too bad. Did you know the Priest maybe? I don't mean an actual priest. That was just what we called him, the Priest. He even let me call him that, though I was a lot younger than him. A welder, he was. We worked on a building site together. Because I was thinking that if we found some people we knew in common, maybe we'd find ourselves too, the two of us, at some time or other, some place or other. I sometimes think of somebody I used to know, and he leads me right away to some other person I knew, then that person leads to someone else, and so on. And I'll be honest, there are times I find it hard to believe I used to know one guy or another. But I must have, since they remember meeting me someplace, at such-and-such a time. One guy, it even turned out we'd played in the same band years ago, him on the trombone, me on the sax. Though he's dead now. But people we know can lead us all kinds of ways, even to places we'd never want to go.

One guy abroad told me about these two brothers he used to know who'd fought on opposite sides in a civil war. Brothers on opposite sides, you can imagine what ruthless enemies they must have made. But the war was ruthless too. People killed each other like they wanted to drown each other in blood. Civil wars are much worse than ordinary wars, as you know. Because there's no greater hatred than the kind that comes from closeness. So when the war ended they continued to be enemies. They lived in the same village, but they wouldn't allow their wives to talk to one another, or their children to play together. And it goes without saying that they themselves never spoke a word to each other. But they both used to go to the same bar. It was another matter that there was only one bar in the village. They'd sit at separate tables, drink their beer, read the paper. If there was only one newspaper, when one of them finished reading it he'd put it back where he got it, even if his brother's table was nearer. The other one did the same thing if he was the first one to read it.

But the one who finished reading first didn't leave. He went on drinking his beer, as if he was waiting for his brother to finish reading. Almost every day they'd show up at more or less the same time, as if they knew when they were supposed to come. They drank their beer, read the paper, the second one after the first one or the first one after the second one, then when their glasses were empty they'd leave. The second one after the first one or the first one after the second one, just the same. It never happened that one of them finished his beer sooner and left. They didn't have to sneak glances, you could easily see the beer in their glasses. Or maybe because they were brothers they had the same rhythm? In any case they drank at the same pace. And that seemed to show they hadn't stopped being brothers. Because as for words, the war had killed the words in both of them for good.

The years passed and they got older. One of them went gray, the other one lost his hair, and they kept coming to the bar, one of them at one table, the other one at the other, they drank their beer and read the newspaper. And each time they'd put it back where they got it. They needed eyeglasses to read now, and they weren't that steady on their feet. But neither of them would give the paper to the other one when he was done with it. Then they'd finish their beer, one of them would leave and the other one would leave right after. All those years, neither of them said so much as:

"Here, here's your paper."

That one sentence might have been enough. Because who knows if with that single sentence they wouldn't have said everything they hadn't said to each other all those years. You can fit an awful lot into one sentence. Maybe everything. Maybe a whole lifetime. A sentence is the measure of the world, a philosopher once said. That's right, the same one. I sometimes wonder if the reason we have to say so many words throughout our life might be in order for that one sentence to emerge from among them. What sentence? Everyone has their own. One that you could utter in a fit of despair and not be lying. At least to yourself.

If only you'd known the Priest. You know, the welder. I couldn't tell you. I don't even know what his first name was. Everyone always just said, the Priest. His first name and last name got lost somewhere along the way. You know what, you even resemble him a bit, now that I look at you. Hand to God. There's something of him in your features, in your eyes. Of course, I mean when you were younger, as I imagine you. He was still young then too. A lot older than me, but I was no more than a kid back then. It was only my second building site, and I worked on the first one less than a year. When you lift your head a bit that way it's like I was looking at him. Stop shelling a moment. When your hands stop moving your face is clearer. Now I'm not so sure. Maybe a little.

Why Priest? He'd trained to be a priest, spent three years in seminary, but he gave it up. That he never told me. But he kept his surplice and stole, and his Bible, he had them in a separate little suitcase that he kept locked. Though on a building site like that, who wouldn't open another person's suitcase and take a look inside? Especially one that was locked. Before he went to sleep he'd always kneel by his bed and pray for a long time. He never missed Sunday Mass. So it was all the more of a temptation to open the suitcase. Work on the building site often continued on a Sunday, especially if it was running behind, but he always had to go to Mass.

Of course he got into trouble, he was written up, they docked his bonuses. At the worksite meetings they claimed it was because of people like him that the building was behind schedule. That there were too many believers on the site, and he was an example to them. Though he was no exception. All kinds of people worked on building sites in those days. Building sites were like hiding places. So if they'd wanted to get rid of all those of one kind or another, there wouldn't have been anyone left to do the job. Not to mention the fact that there'd have been no tradesmen whatsoever. And he was one of the best welders. Maybe even the best of all. All the other welders would go to him for advice. Plus, he was hard-working. If there was some urgent job that needed doing he wouldn't leave the site till it was done, even if he had to work through the night. He didn't drink, didn't smoke, didn't go to dances. He kept away from girls. In his spare time he read. In that respect he was an exception, because everyone else drank in their spare time. Even before he went to sleep, however exhausted he was, he'd always say he had to take up his book and read at least a couple of pages. One time when I'd climbed the scaffolding to where he was, he said to me that books are the only way for a human not to forget that he's a human. Him, in any case, he couldn't live without books. Books are a world too, a world that you choose for yourself, not the one you've come into.

He kept trying to persuade me, till in the end I started reading too. I thought to myself, it's no skin off my nose, I'll give it a try, especially because I liked him. He'd asked me one time if I wouldn't like to read a book. I was reluctant, said I had to do this and that, I didn't have time. In the end, just to please him I told him to bring me something. He had a few books, he kept them in another suitcase, that one he didn't keep locked so no one looked in it. And that was how things began. There was a second book, a third. Then he said there weren't any more books for me, because the ones he had would be too difficult. So he took me to the library. There was a little library on the site, a few shelves. He poked about and in the end he picked out something for me. When I'd finished it he went back with me and chose something else. Let me tell you, out of respect for him I eventually started to read of my own free will. And like him, before I went to sleep I had to read at least a few pages.

It's strange you didn't know him. Everyone on the site knew him, he was well liked. He was always impartial and fair. Well-disposed towards everyone. He'd stop and talk with each person. Even if he was in a hurry he'd at least ask you about this or that. And he always remembered when something had been bothering you the last time you spoke to him. He'd lend you a few *zloties* if you needed it. If a cat or a dog wandered onto the site, he'd feed them. And the best proof of what a good welder he was is that he worked on the highest places. When a building was going up he'd always be at the very top. He was never secured. Never held on to anything. He didn't even turn off his torch as he moved from one joint to another. He walked across the girders like an acrobat. And you have to know that the higher up the work, the better a welder you have to be.

Sometimes he'd look down from way up there and see me crossing the yard, and he'd call to me to come up to him for a moment because there was something he wanted to tell me. I'd go up there if I didn't have anything urgent on. He liked me, I couldn't say why. I was just a kid compared to him. He said it was a good excuse for a break when I went to see him. No, it wasn't like we talked about anything special. He'd ask me if I'd finished the book he picked out for me last time at the library, if I'd liked it, what I thought about it. It wasn't that he was checking whether I'd read it, rather if I'd got it. He guided me in how to understand it. He'd relate it to different things, life, the world, people in general. And always in the course of things he'd say something that made me think for a long time afterwards.

We didn't only talk about books. He'd say that it was only here, up at a height, that we can feel human. That was a truth I only grasped much, much later. Especially because down below people mostly didn't talk, there the work hurried you all day long, or you were driven crazy because they hadn't delivered some materials or other and the work was at a standstill. Unless it was over vodka, but then you had to watch who you drank with, because they'd sometimes snitch on you. Actually, they also snitched on you when you didn't talk. Even if all you did was let out a sigh. He said that on all the building sites he'd been on, he always worked as high up as he could get. And since he'd worked on so many sites, the high places were sort of his territory, so it was no surprise that it was up there he most liked talking. Down

6

below, when he came down after work, he read, fed the dogs and the cats, and he didn't keep company with anyone. Despite the fact that, like I said, everyone liked him. Naturally he earned a lot more working up there. But it wasn't about the money for him.

So can you imagine it, one day during lunch, word went around that the Priest had fallen to his death. Some people said he'd fallen, others that someone else must have had a hand in it, still others that he'd fallen deliberately. Otherwise he would have been holding his torch and had his goggles on. Whereas he'd set the torch aside and taken his goggles off. But we never learned the truth. The cause of it may have been concealed up above there. The construction had already reached the fifth floor. And the floors were high ones, the building was going to be a factory. When you get used to the high places like that, maybe you can't get over the fact that you live down below. With high places there's no messing around. Me too, whenever I climbed up to visit with him, I always felt something either pulling me downwards, or drawing me even higher.

If you ask me, though, the truth lay elsewhere. There was a girl. She worked in the cafeteria. No, nothing of that sort. I told you he kept away from girls. He liked her, the feeling was mutual. He was gentle, polite, not like the rest of us. The most he did was when she'd bring the soup or the main course, he'd admire her braided hair, say how beautiful it was, how you hardly ever saw hair like that anymore. It was true, her braid was as thick as my wrist here. And it reached all the way down past her waist at the back. Everyone would tug at it as she brought their food.

Not me. For some reason I was too shy. Besides, I'd only recently come to work on the site. When she put my soup or main course in front of me I didn't even look at her, I only ever saw her from a distance. The other guys had known her for a long time. She'd gotten used to having her braid pulled. I won't lie, I liked the look of her from the start. And she knew it right away. One time she leaned over to my ear and whispered, You should tug on my braid too, see what it feels like. I didn't. But I decided that even without that, she'd still be mine. When the right moment came I'd tell her. For the while I didn't let anything show. I never even said to her, You look nice today Miss Basia, or Basieńka—Barbara was her name. Though everyone said that to her every day. When she brought me my plate I'd say, Thank you. That was it. Other guys, they wouldn't have been able to eat if they hadn't pulled at her braid or at least said, You look nice today Miss Basia, or Basieńka.

Sometimes she'd spill the soup because someone tugged at her braid before she'd had time to put the bowl down. Plus, some of them had hands twice the size of yours or mine, rugged and strong. She'd even break a plate at times trying to free herself from a hand like that. A good few plates or bowls got broken because of that braid of hers. Same when she was clearing the empty plates away.

One day she was carrying plates with the main course on a tray, six plates if I remember correctly, when someone grabbed her braid, even though she wasn't going to his table, she was just passing by. The tray wobbled in her hands and all the plates crashed to the floor. They were going to fire her on the spot. Luckily the guy did the right thing and paid for all the plates and all the food. After that the men were more careful, they only tugged at her braid once she'd put the plates on the table, otherwise every last plate would have gotten broken, and not through any fault of hers. Unless you could blame the braid. If you ask me, girls or women who work in cafeterias, especially on building sites like that, they shouldn't be too good-looking. Nice, polite, of course, but not too good-looking.

Sometimes she'd wear her braid up on her head in a bun. Maybe it was for self-protection, because how else can you protect yourself when you've got the kind of braid that just begs to be grabbed and held for at least a moment. Or perhaps she wanted to look nicer, who can tell. Though in my book she had no need to look nicer. Without the braid, though, she looked quite different, she became kind of unapproachable, haughty. When she put the bowl or the plate in front of you, she seemed to be doing you a favor. I didn't like the bun. I thought to myself, when she's my wife I'll tell her I prefer the braid. With the braid, when it swung back and forth behind her back she looked, I don't know how to put it, like she'd only just risen into the world.

You're smiling . . . my imagination's a bit old-fashioned, right? But that was how I felt back then. Though if you think about it, don't you reckon we continue to imagine things the way people have imagined them? However much the world changes. However different we are. Or maybe we just pretend to be different so we can keep up with the world. While in our innermost longings we're all still the same, we just hide it from ourselves and the rest of the world.

Besides, tell me yourself, can anyone imagine nicer hair on a girl than a braid? Naturally, for a braid like that you need a mass of hair, and not the thin kind. You need hair that's a gift, as they used to say in my childhood. Here, on the lake, in the season, when people come on a Saturday or Sunday or on vacation, you sometimes see nice hair. But it's best not to look too closely. It's all dyed, and often colors that you never see in real hair. Real hair has a different color on each person, have you ever noticed that? In addition to which, their hair looks like it's been all puffed up by hairdressers, with all those conditioners and shampoos and gels. Often their heads look like bunches of flowers. And the whole bunch could fit in your hand if you plucked it from their head.

In general, something wrong is going on with people's hair. Maybe it's a sign that something bad is starting to happen in the world? Despite what you might think, more often than not the beginning is hard to spot. It's rare for anything to start with big things or big events. It's usually from something little, often something insignificant, like people's hair for example. But have you noticed that more and more young men are bald? And they're getting younger and younger. When I was their age everyone had a shock of hair.

When you only look at people's hair, or for example only at their bare feet, for instance here at the lake, or only at their hands, their eyes, their mouths, their eyebrows, you see them altogether differently than when you look at them as a whole. It gives you all kinds of insights. It gives you lots to think about.

It was that braid of hers that was the start of what came next. Though no one suspected it could be the braid. A braid is just a braid. It was tempting to grab it and feel it, that was all. Though let me tell you, when it sometimes accidentally brushed against my face as she was clearing plates from the table, it gave me goose bumps, as if death had brushed against me. Though I couldn't have imagined her with any other hair.

Actually, there was something odd about her in general. When they took hold of her braid she'd always blush, when she should have been accustomed to it by then. She'd served so many meals, there'd been so many lunches since the building site was set up, she ought to have gotten used to it. But she blushed even when someone just looked her in the eye when she was bringing the plates. She'd blush whenever someone said, You look nice today, Miss Basia, or Basieńka. She always looked nice, but they'd say that to her. I mean, there just aren't that many words you can use when you want to say something nice to a girl, especially in a cafeteria, when she's giving you your soup or your main course or clearing the dishes away.

It's another matter that as far as words are concerned, something has happened between men and women, don't you think? Someone here said to me once that words are unnecessary, that they're dying out. It's obvious what a man is, what a woman is, what do you need words for. True or false ones, wise or unwise, elegant or clumsy, either way they all lead without exception to the same thing. So what are they for?

True, on the building sites things weren't that great either when it came to words. You used them as much as was needed on the construction. And you can imagine what kinds of words they were mostly. One job followed another, so you just dropped by the cafeteria to quickly eat your lunch and then hurry back to work. You were dirty and sweaty, you didn't even wash your hands sometimes. Plus, while you were eating there were other men waiting for your place the moment you were done. Where could you be expected to learn other words? You look nice today, Miss Basia, or Basieńka, that was all some of them could manage. And those were the ones we reckoned knew how to talk. It was much simpler to just grab hold of her braid.

Were any of them in love with her? I can't speak for the others. Probably all of them would gladly have gone to bed with her. But were any of them in love with her? As far as true love is concerned, not many people are capable of that, as you know. It's hard to find, especially on a building site.

The construction wasn't finished, it was three-quarters done at most, when here the machinery started arriving from abroad, in accordance with the plan. Soon after that a crew came to install it, including a couple of men who worked for the foreign company that had sent the machinery. It looked like they wouldn't have a whole lot to do for the moment, but they suddenly got all busy. They told us to quickly finish off one of the shops and began installing some of the machines. Luckily for us they had to redo the measurements, because something had come out wrong, they even had to redraw their plans, and that gave us time to catch up with our own schedule. They were constantly sitting around the table in management, adjusting, arguing, threatening, saying it was supposed to be this way and not that.

They were classy guys. Every second one was a qualified engineer. A whole separate barracks was prepared for them to stay in. They even started calling it a pavilion instead of a barracks. They plastered the outside, painted the interior, weather-stripped it, put in new doors and windows. Each of them had his own room. Those of us who'd been living in that barracks before, they moved us to private lodgings, cramming seven or eight guys into one room. They bought the newcomers shiny new furniture, big wide beds, plus sofas, armchairs, wardrobes, tables, stools, bookshelves, bedside tables, night lights, lace curtains in the windows, drapes. There weren't many private homes that were as nice as those rooms. Also, in each room there was a radio, a rug on the floor, a mirror on the wall.

When we lived in that barracks, we had iron bunk beds and one wardrobe between six of us. The most you could do was hang your suit in there if you had one. You kept the rest of your things in a suitcase under your bed, or in old cookie boxes or cigarette cartons. No one would have dreamed of putting drapes on our windows, let alone lace curtains. It was difficult enough to get your turn at the soap or the towel. We bought a piece of calico and hung it over the window on nails at night. Or a mirror. The only mirrors were in the shared bathroom, nearly all of them cracked. Most of the time you had to use a cracked mirror to shave, brush your hair, or for example to squeeze your zits, or tie your necktie on a Sunday. And if you just wanted to take a look at yourself, you looked like you were made of broken pieces like the mirror. In the cafeteria they gave the new guys a separate area by the windows—that was where they had their tables. However late they came, those tables were always free and waiting for them. No one else dared sit there. There were times when all the other tables were occupied, and however much you were in a hurry because you were in the middle of an urgent job, you still had to wait till someone finished eating, even though those other tables were free. And often it wasn't just one or two of us, there'd be a dozen or more guys hovering over the ones who were eating. We'd even tell them to get a move on, eat faster, as a result of which some of them would deliberately draw out their meal. It was infuriating, here your stomach was rumbling, here there was work to do, and right in front of you there were empty tables, almost taunting you. On top of that, often they only showed up when the last men were eating, any number of us could have eaten at their tables in the mean-time. It sometimes happened that someone couldn't wait and went back to work without getting their lunch. At most they'd grab some herring or an egg from the snack bar, or a bit of sausage, though they didn't often have sausage, and they'd go back to work still half hungry.

And just imagine, she fell in love with one of the guys from those tables. In front of everyone, on the very first day. He came in, sat down, and she served him his soup. He looked at her, and she didn't blush, she just looked back at him. For a moment they looked at each other like that, and the whole cafeteria stopped eating for a second. Even if someone was lifting a spoonful of soup to their mouth, or a fork with potatoes or meat, they froze and watched. All the time they'd been grabbing her braid and saying, You look nice today Miss Basia, or Basieńka, and here some complete stranger had shown up and she wasn't even blushing.

He was holding his spoon also, but he hadn't yet put it in his soup, as if he couldn't tear his eyes away from her as she stood over him, or maybe he'd lost his appetite. She couldn't take her eyes off him either. Even though she'd put his soup down in front of him and she should have gone away, the way she'd go away from each of us after she put our soup down. She only snapped out of it when the cook leaned through the kitchen hatch and shouted:

Wiesław Myśliwski

"Basia, don't just stand there! These bowls need taking!"

She said to him:

"I hope you like it."

She'd never said that to any of us.

He said:

"Thank you. I'm sure I will."

And he watched her walk away, right till she reached the hatch. He ate his soup, but it was like he wasn't eating. It was *krupnik*, barley soup, I remember. Do you like *krupnik*? Me, I can't stand it. Ever since I was a kid I've hated it. Eating a bowl of *krupnik* was torture for me. Then she brought him the main course, and he didn't so much as glance at the plate. He took her braid in his hand, but not the way the others would grab hold of it. Rather, he lifted it up on his outspread palm as if he was weighing it to see if by any chance it was made of gold. She didn't snatch it back the way she did with the other men.

"Where on earth do braids like this grow?" he said.

Which of us would have known to say something like that, where do braids like that grow. But she didn't blush. She looked at him as if it was all the same to her what he did with her braid, as if she'd let him do anything he wanted with it.

He could have wrapped it around his neck, he could have cut himself a length of it, he could have unbraided it, she wouldn't have pulled it away. She only said:

"Please eat, sir. Your food'll get cold."

He said:

"I like cold food."

That was another way he was different from the rest of us, none of us would have said we liked cold food. With us, if something wasn't hot enough we'd make a fuss about it on the spot:

"Why is this soup cold? These potatoes look like leftovers! What kind of meat is this, it's bad enough it's offcuts! Miss Basia, tell them in the kitchen there! Take my plate back, have them heat it up!"

Whereas he'd said he liked cold food. He was on a building site, in the cafeteria, and he liked cold food. I don't know if anyone enjoyed their meal that day. I couldn't even tell you what the main course was. Probably meatballs, because we mostly got meatballs. They were more breadcrumbs than meat, but they were called meatballs.

You probably think she drove a dagger into my heart, as they say. Well, it did hurt. I didn't finish my main course. I went back to work. Though I didn't much feel like working either. In the end I made myself feel better by saying I'd wait him out. They'd install all the machinery in the cold storage plant and he'd leave, and I'd still be there. I just had to be patient. Besides, I found it hard to believe it could have happened just like that on the first day. She'd given him his soup and his main course, and that was that.

But from that day she changed beyond recognition. She looked and she didn't see. Even when you said to her, Good morning, Miss Basia, or Basieńka, sometimes she didn't answer. When she gave us our plates it seemed like it was all the same to her which of us was which. She knew the cafeteria like the back of her hand, she could have found her way among the tables blindfold, but she began to make mistakes. The next table had been waiting longer than us, but she served us first. She'd never gotten the order wrong before. She knew virtually to the second who had arrived first, who had sat where. The opposite happened too. We'd be calling, over here, Miss Basia, or Basieńka, we were here before them. She'd give us a distracted glance and serve the guys who'd come after us. Or she'd bring the main course to a table where they hadn't had their soup yet, while there were other men waiting for their main course at a table that was even closer to her.

It's possible to fall in love at first sight, but to that extent? It was enough to see what happened when he showed up in the cafeteria. If she was carrying bowls or plates to some table, the tray would shake in her hands, the plates would clink, then when she served them it was like she wanted to chuck them all down at once. And right away she'd run to the hatch for his soup. He'd still be eating the soup and already she'd be bringing him his main course. While us, when we finished our soup we always had to wait for the main course till she was done serving everyone their soup. Sometimes we'd even tap our forks against our bowls because we'd been waiting too long for the main course. Him, he never had to wait.

You should have seen her when he didn't show up at the usual time. You'd have thought it wasn't her that was serving the meals, her hands were doing the job all alone. As for her, she didn't even see what her hands were carrying. She was just one big tormented waiting mass. Here she'd be putting plates down on the tables, but her eyes would be fixed on the door. I'm telling you, when you ate you could virtually feel that torment of hers in the spoons and forks and knives.

Suddenly he'd appear. We'd be bent over our food, no one was looking at the door, but everyone would know from her reaction that he had come in. Right away she'd perk up, smile. Like she'd come back to life. Her braid would swing. Her eyes would sparkle. She'd almost be dancing among the tables. You had the impression she was all set to tear the braid off her head, put it in a vase and stand it on the table in front of him to make his meal more enjoyable.

And all that was only what you could see in the cafeteria. You'd often meet them walking along, their fingers interlocked. Or he'd have his arm around her, and she'd be pressing against him. When someone nodded to say hello, he'd nod back for both of them, because she wouldn't see. I have to admit he had good manners. He didn't put on airs. Whenever he needed my help as an electrician, or someone else's, he'd always wait till you finished what you were doing, then ask politely. He knew how to make people like him. And honestly, we even did like him.

Her, on the other hand, she seemed to be getting more and more impatient. She'd clear up in the cafeteria, but for example in the kitchen she wouldn't want to wash the dishes because she was in a hurry. Then later you'd see her waiting somewhere for him to get off work. Mostly she'd pace up and down on the other side of the street from the building site. Or even along the perimeter, right outside the chain-link fence. Though there was no path, just mounds of earth dumped there for the purposes of the site. She just walked back and forth on those mounds, sometimes holding on to the fence. When she saw him coming she'd run so fast her braid would bounce up and down. Sometimes she'd take off her shoes and run barefoot so she wouldn't miss him. If it was too far to go around by the gate, she'd squeeze through the nearest hole in the fence. There were all kinds of holes, people used them to thieve things from the site.

However long it took him to get off work, she'd wait. Everyone knows you can't always clock off at the time you're supposed to. All the more so on a building site like that, especially when you're behind schedule. Plus, they were on a foreign contract. We weren't, but even in our case you rarely got off when you were meant to. When things really fell behind, no one counted the hours.

She waited even when it was raining. She got herself a little umbrella, or perhaps he bought it for her. And even when it was pouring she'd wait under her umbrella. Or by a wall under the eaves, or in the watchman's hut by the gate when the rain was really heavy. You'd sometimes see her in the library too. I'd go there to get something to read, and here I'd see her at a table by the window with a book, and the window would just happen to look out onto the site. But she never glanced up to see who'd come in. Not many people visited the library. So the librarian loved it when anyone appeared. But her, she didn't look up. She even seemed to sink deeper into her book, so as not to draw attention to herself.

So I would not notice her. Or God forbid I should ever ask what she was reading. That might have embarrassed her, turned her against me, hurt her even. And what for? I knew she was waiting for him. And who cares what she was reading. It was better she was in the library than standing or pacing to and fro in the rain. You know, I often felt more sorry for her than I did for myself.

It goes without saying that people told all kinds of stories about her. I don't even want to repeat them. For instance, there were rumors that she cleaned his room, did his laundry, washed his shirts, darned his socks. That she spent the night there. See how her eyes are all puffy, what do you think that's from? It never occurred to anyone it could be from crying. It was like that love of hers was the property of everyone. Like anybody had the right to walk all over her love the way you walked about the site, trampling it, even tossing down your cigarette butt. All because she served in the cafeteria.

No one said anymore, You look nice today Miss Basia, or Basieńka, she couldn't look nice with her eyes swollen. They said she'd lost her looks, she'd gone to the dogs, that her braid wasn't what it used to be, or her eyes. Maybe she was pregnant, she moved more slowly now, she wasn't so brisk when she brought you your meal. They said various things. Someone supposedly even overheard her say to him, You promised. To which he answered, We'll do it. You just have to understand. She says, What do I have to understand? I'm not as dumb as you think I am. Just because I work in a cafeteria? And she burst into tears.

The librarian, though, she was easy on her, she was an older woman and she'd probably been through a lot herself. Even after it was time to close up the library she'd keep it open if it was raining outside and the other woman was still sitting over her book. She'd tidy the books on the shelves, replace torn slip covers, catalogue new items.

Sometimes though, despite the rain she'd suddenly give back her book and leave as if something had agitated her, and at most the librarian would say to her:

"It's good you have an umbrella, Miss Basia."

She'd apologize to the librarian, explain that she'd just remembered she had something urgent to do.

"Never mind, never mind, Miss Basia. I understand, it happens. I'll just put a bookmark at your page. I'll leave the book over here, it'll be waiting for you."

"Oh, please do. Thank you." And she'd almost rush out, as if she really had remembered some pressing errand.

Then a moment later you'd see her somewhere by the fence, waiting for him. And the librarian would also see her from the window. Or she'd ask the watchmen to let her in to the site, and she'd wait there. She'd sometimes be wandering around till evening, till nighttime if he didn't show up. When someone came by she'd slip behind a crane or a backhoe, or behind a pile of bricks, some reels of cable, a heap of crates or barrels or used tires, there were mountains of stuff like that all over the main yard. Wherever she could hide.

Why would she hide when everyone knew anyway? Exactly. I wondered about that myself. Especially because I often used to run into her myself on the site in the evening. Though she hid from me too. Maybe that was the nature of her love, that it was somehow at odds with the world. Or maybe she wanted it to be that way.

In the end they got married. It was a strange wedding. It wasn't a civil one, but it also wasn't in a church. Apparently he'd so turned her head that she agreed to have the Priest marry them. That's right, the welder. She had wanted a church wedding. He wouldn't agree, because as he explained to her, he could lose his job over it. As she knew, he was on a foreign contract, and he needed the backing of important people. He couldn't even tell her who, it was an official secret. Besides, what difference did it make whether it was in a church or not. The main thing was that they should be married by a priest. A church was just where there was a priest. And she knew him after all. And the fact that he was a welder, what of it? He was a priest. People found themselves in various situations these days, even priests. He had a surplice and stole, and a Bible, he kept them in a suitcase, what could they be for other than to perform services? He'd be sure to agree. He knew what times were like. And he'd certainly keep their secret. Because for the moment it had to be a secret. At most he'd invite three or four of his closest friends. They wouldn't breathe a word of it, he guaranteed. She shouldn't invite anyone from her side, not her father or mother, no one.

They agreed on a Saturday evening when the site would be deserted, so no one would see it. A lot of people working on the site would leave after work on Saturday to travel to their families. The watchmen at the gatehouse would get a bottle of vodka so they wouldn't see anything or hear anything. Just in case, he'd tell them it was his birthday. They'd cover the window, the table would serve as an altar, they'd cover it with a white cloth. He'd buy candles. It would be good to have a crucifix, he didn't know if the Priest had one. Maybe she had one at home, she should bring it. But she should make sure no one saw her. So she did. Do you think she was being gullible? I doubt it. Desire is stronger than suspicion.

She wanted a wedding dress, a white one, because she'd always dreamed of getting married in a white dress with a train. He gave it some thought. No problem, she'd have one, he'd buy it for her. He'd go into town and buy it. She didn't have to go with him. He'd get her the most beautiful one, the most expensive one. If she went with him someone might twig. She shouldn't worry, it would be the right size. It'd fit her like a glove. How tall was she exactly? That's what he thought. And her hips and waist, and here? That's what he thought. So why did she need to go? What if someone saw them together in the store, and her trying on a wedding dress, then there'd be problems. It wasn't their fault they were living in such times. He wished they'd met in a different age. But she herself could see it was best if he went alone. White shoes? He'd buy her white shoes. What size was she? That's what he thought. Just in case, she should draw the outline of her foot on a sheet of paper. That way he'd be more confident. Especially since with shoes it can happen that even though they're the right size, they turn out to be too tight or too loose. Would she also like white gloves? He could get her some white gloves while he was about it. What else would she like?

How do I know all this? You've never worked on a building site? Then you don't know much about life. On a building site everyone knows everything. You don't even need to eavesdrop. You don't need to see, you don't need to guess. You could say that what happens, what's said, what someone feels, what they think about, that first off everyone knows it. Then what comes next only confirms it.

Anyhow, she didn't want any white gloves, because why should he spend more money on gloves. No, she didn't want gloves. It was going to be an expensive enough business as it was. The dress alone, you say it'll be the most beautiful one, the most expensive one. Then how much will the shoes cost? Plus, she'd never seen anyone get married in gloves. She used to go to nearly every wedding at her church. Every wedding kind of changed her life for a moment. She'd gone since she was a girl. Even when it was total strangers getting married, she'd still go. When old people got married there was never much of a crowd, but she would be there. So what if they were old? It was still a wedding. And when they promised they'd never leave each other she would feel her heart pounding in her chest, tears welling in her eyes. But she'd never seen a bride in gloves. I mean, they had to put rings on their fingers, and what, was she supposed to take off a glove at that moment?

All of a sudden she realized he'd forgotten about the rings. He had to buy rings. He didn't have to because he already had them. He'd thought ahead. He took them out and unwrapped them, told her to try one on. How did he know it would be the right size for her finger? If it didn't fit this finger it would go on that one. Try it on. If it's too big, later on we'll give it to a jeweler and have it made smaller. If it's too small, she can put it on her pinkie finger for now. Later on we'll give it to a jeweler and have it enlarged. He'd bought them some time ago, before he was working on the foreign contract. An opportunity had come along when someone lost at cards and didn't have anything else to pay with.

No, he didn't play cards, not him. He'd bought them off the guy that lost. He'd figured they might come in handy. And they had. He'd forgotten about them, it was only when he saw her in the cafeteria that he remembered he had them. It was like those rings had chosen her to be his wife. Though they wouldn't be able to wear them for the moment. After the wedding they'd take them off and he'd keep them safe. Once his contract was over they could put them back on. Maybe they'd go away somewhere. Maybe abroad. He'd try and pull some strings in the foreign company whose machinery they were installing.

Who wouldn't have swallowed it all, you tell me. Common sense might have made her suspicious. But common sense always loses out to life. She was working in a cafeteria, and bam. Soup, main course, bam. Anyone who wanted could grab hold of her braid, but he lifted it on his outspread palm and weighed it to see if it was maybe made of gold. Common sense tells you to be wary of any love, because you never know where it might lead you. Common sense tells you you should be wary of yourself. But it isn't people that create common sense for themselves. And what is common sense anyway? You tell me that. And I'll tell you back that no one could survive in life by just following common sense. Common sense is all well and good. . . . But all it really is, is what you say when you don't know what else to say.

It's too bad you didn't know him, you could've warned her. You didn't know him? Though she wouldn't have believed you anyway, of that I'm sure. No one can ever be drawn away from love. And if you ask me, they shouldn't be. When someone's drawn away you never know where they'll end up.

I thought the Priest might not agree. But they made him. Is it so hard to force a man to go against himself? We go against ourselves all the time just to avoid trouble. They forced him to do it by saying they'd put the word out. I told you he kept away from girls. No, that no one knew. There has to be something you don't know even when you know everything. He'd quit seminary, that much was known. He kept a surplice and stole and a Bible in a suitcase, that much was known. Before he started his lunch in the cafeteria he would cross himself, he prayed every evening before he went to bed, he never missed Sunday Mass, so everyone thought he still kept up his calling. Even I didn't know, and we'd often had long conversations together when I climbed to where he was working up aloft. How did the other man know? I couldn't say. I don't want to make accusations without any proof. In any case, if word had gotten around, his life on the site would have been miserable. It wouldn't have made any difference that he was one of the best welders, in fact the very best. And it would have followed him to other sites. He would never have gotten his life back.

They covered the window just like he said. What it looked like inside, we only knew from what one of the watchmen said. The other watchmen had sent him from the watch house to ask for another bottle, because they'd finished what they'd been given. But the moment he crossed the threshold they stuck the bottle in his hand and pushed him back out the door. So he didn't get to see if the table was covered with a white cloth, whether candles were lit, whether there was a crucifix. All he saw was that they were all drunk, especially her. He didn't see if the Priest was there. Maybe he left right after the wedding. Though it would have been strange if he hadn't gotten drunk too.

Besides, what could a watchman like that actually see when he was drunk himself, and every drunk thinks that it's other people who are drunk, not him. The watchmen had supposedly been given a crate of vodka, and they'd drunk the whole lot when they sent him out for another bottle. You can imagine how far gone he was. The watchmen were like that. They had uniforms and rifles, but things were always getting pinched from the site. One time someone even stole a tractor. And they didn't see a thing. So how could you believe him? But he said what he said, and other people repeated his words after him.

In any case, after the wedding bad things started happening between them. Him, he didn't even look up when she served him his soup or his main course in the cafeteria. And as for her, it no longer made a difference whether she was putting the food in front of him or someone else. Her eyes seemed to be losing their shine from one day to the next. You couldn't say, You look nice today, Miss Basia, or Basieńka, because she looked like she might burst into tears. She unbraided her hair and just tied it behind with a ribbon. It still looked nice, but it wasn't the same as when she'd worn the braid. But no one had the courage to ask her why she'd done it.

The Priest stopped coming to the cafeteria, and that made you wonder as well. Apparently he went to some tavern to eat. Then one day she happened to be bringing the main course to the table where I was sitting when someone ran in to say that the Priest had fallen from the scaffolding.

Either he'd fallen or it was something else, in any case the guy shouted to the whole cafeteria that he'd fallen. She had one more plate to put on the table and, as chance would have it it was mine. The plate fell from her hands to the floor. She burst out crying, covered her face with her hands and ran into the kitchen. What went on in there I couldn't tell you. But people in the cafeteria could have thought it was because of the dropped plate.

We all rushed to the door, people came hurrying from the offices and from management, everyone was running, a crowd gathered and it was hard to push through to the place where he'd fallen. Someone checked his pulse and his heart, but he was dead. Soon an ambulance came, the police, they started questioning people and asking about witnesses. But it wasn't by accident that it had happened at lunchtime, if you ask me.

I didn't see her again that day. And him, he left that same evening. For the next few days she didn't work in the cafeteria. One of the cooks took her place. They said she'd taken some sick days, but she'd be back soon. And she did come back. Only, you wouldn't have recognized her. She took soup to the men from the foreign contract and right away she asked them when he was coming back. They didn't say anything. She brought them their main course and asked again when he would be coming back. Then, when they still said nothing, she made such a scene that they got up and left. She was crying and shouting that they'd come to get their meal and they'd left him to do all the work. He'd get exhausted working so much. As it was he didn't look well. He was pale, he'd lost weight. The next day she was fired.

After that, from time to time she'd come to the cafeteria, stand by the hatch and say to the cooks that she just wanted to serve him his meal when he came. And the cooks, like you'd expect with cooks, they'd say to her, Come in to the kitchen, sit yourself down, we'll tell you when he comes and you can serve him, we can see the door from here, when he comes in we'll let you know.

You'd also meet her outside the gate waiting for him to get off work. Everyone had already left, but she'd sometimes wait till dusk, till night. It would be raining, pouring even, but she'd wait. She didn't have her umbrella anymore, who knew what had happened to it. Out of pity the watchmen would sometimes bring her in to the watch house so she wouldn't get so wet. Or they'd tell her to go away, that there was no point in waiting.

"My husband works here," she would reply.

"He used to, but he doesn't anymore. And what do you mean, your husband?"

"He's my husband, he took an oath. I wore a wedding gown, a priest married us."

"What do you mean, a priest. He was a welder. Besides, he's dead now."

Sometimes she'd beg them to let her onto the site.

"Let me in."

"Come to your senses, girl."

"I'll just tell him I'm waiting for him."

Occasionally they'd let her in. If not, she'd squeeze through a hole in the fence. She knew all the holes, after all. Even when they saw her wandering around the site they didn't drive her off. They turned a blind eye. If someone from management had seen her they had a good excuse, that they'd not let her in through the main gate. Besides, she was quiet, all she did was walk around the main yard. She never stopped anyone, never asked any questions. If someone came along she wouldn't hide anymore. No one asked her any questions either, everyone knew. Sometimes she'd sit down somewhere and lose herself in thought, like she didn't even know where she was.

From time to time I'd cross paths with her when I happened to work late on the site. One time it was almost evening, she was sitting on a crate.

"Oh, Miss Basia," I said.

"It's not 'miss' anymore," she said. "I'm married. Who are you?"

"An electrician, Miss Basia."

"Oh, right. I remember you from the cafeteria. I used to think you were cute. You were a shy one, I remember. You used to want me to be your wife. A lot of them did."

She surprised me, I'd never told her that. I wanted to say to her it wasn't that I used to want her to be my wife, I still did now. You might not believe it, but I suddenly felt like I wanted to be in her unhappiness with her. True love is a wound. You can only find it inside yourself when someone else's pain hurts you like your own.

But before I could explain this to her she said:

"Except that you guys working on building sites, wherever your site is, that's where your wife is. What do you know about love."

My courage failed me.

"Help me find my way out of here."

"The gate's over there," I said. "I'll walk you out."

"I don't want to use the gate." She looked at me as if with those old eyes from the cafeteria. "You know, I still think you're cute. But I already have a husband."

The King of Golden Silk

(poem)

AURÉLIA LASSAQUE

Aurélia Lassaque was born in 1983 and lives in southwestern France. She is keenly interested in the relationship between poetry and music and has collaborated internationally with musicians, dancers, and visual artists. Her poems have been translated in more than twenty languages. In 2011 she organized the exhibition *Dialogue entre cultures et langues* for the Council of Europe. She is an adviser of the poetry prize Premio Ostana, Scritture in lingua madre (Italy) and a literary adviser, with Boubacar Boris Diop, of the Festival Paroles Indigo (held in Arles, France). She has dedicated her dissertation to Occitan baroque drama.

According to translator James Thomas, Lassaque is "a leading contemporary voice in Occitan, a language still thought erroneously by many to have died with the last troubadours of the late thirteenth century. . . . [C]ontemporary Occitan literature is still largely a treasure chest awaiting future English translations. . . . Her poetry is characterised by a fascination with human interactions, emotions and the mysteries of the universe, a probing of the possibilities beyond the rituals and repetitions of time and the seasons."

Translated from Occitan by James Thomas.

He ensnares birds and banters with the wind.
Pitched on wild grassland
He's lost his eyes
Stolen from the coat of a soldier.
Three young lads came along
Scattered his guts on the ground
Where they laid a dishevelled girl.

Without his body of golden silk
The scarecrow
Dreams ungovernable dreams
That bewilder the birds.

Her skin, hot and dark
Like a summer's night,
Stretches to catch out the dawn
As her wild-mare body moves,
Uncoiling once more
Probing in the deepness of her limbs
A bird-catcher's paradise.

She spent long secret hours in the orchard
Resting her tongue against russet sap
Seeping from the trees' gaping mouths;
One evening of gathering storms,
A young man from the sea found her
And stole her away on his carnal crown.

Aurélia Lassaque

A black woman dreamed
Of round, red oranges,
A pulpy mirror
Of her breasts, dripping new milk;
She bore a boy
With russet hair and green eyes;
In secret she kept him
In a basket of false fruits.

Beyond green mornings they glided
Over other-worldly waters,
So many times they circled the clearest skies,
Greeted the infinite last gasps of the stars
And returned to meagre fields
In their hundreds
In the muteness of present time,
Birds of pure morning.

Aurélia Lassaque

A house of stone and linen curtains
tinted by rays of light and dust.
The ocean, stretching to the horizon,
peers through the window.
Inside the house, a virginal woman;
her ashen hair, teased by winds from the high seas,
dances with the evening.
On the table,
her old, well-folded trousseau
catches her eye
just as the night birds start to sing.

At the solstice hour
People dressed in wood
Lure into their leafage
Birds without faces.

The wandering stream
Drags towards the shores
Its memories of snow.

My sylvan trees
Have reddened with summer's first day.

The men from the town
Said that was rust
Blown in from Japan.

But they don't know
That the trees in this coomb
In their deepest secret roots
Stroke living stones
That start to dream
That the wind and the rain
Will take them naked on clay
At the solstice hour.

Aurélia Lassaque

You've chosen the path for the land of night.
The desert is made of ice there
And the stars die of boredom.
Stretch out your arms and dig,
Dust will be your bread,
You'll swallow our tears.
Go now, go, and don't return.
If you hear the stones wailing,
The letters of your name are being engraved.

———

Five Fingers

(novel excerpt)

MĀRA ZĀLĪTE

Māra Zālīte was born in 1952 in Krasnoyarsk, Siberia, where her family had been deported by the Soviet regime. When she was four years old, they returned to Latvia. In 1975 she graduated from the Department of Philology at the University of Latvia. She has led the Young Writers' Studio, been editor in chief of the literary magazine *Karogs*, and headed the copyright agency of Latvia. She is the author of five poetry books and twenty-one staged plays and musicals, including several rock librettos, as well as children's books and collections of essays. She was in the forefront of Latvian intellectuals during the so-called Singing Revolution and continues to have a prominent voice in current events.

Five Fingers is her first novel. Told from the point of view of a little girl, it tells of the time her family returned to her grandfather's farm in Latvia, where she had to reconcile the life she found there with the distant fairyland description of Latvia she had heard from her family while in Siberia. This work debuts in English in our pages.

Translated from Latvian by Margita Gailitis; edited by Vija Kostoff.

The Fortune Teller

In the morning Laura has to eat at least a cuckoo's mouthful. Otherwise she can't go outside, because the cuckoo—that's the famine cuckoo—can coo-coo-cuckoo her away. If she'll be coo-cuckooed away, then next year there won't be any mouthfuls, neither a cuckoo's nor a non-cuckoo's. Nor a non-cuckoo's! Laura laughs—that's funny! Mīma is firm about this, laugh or don't laugh, and she herself eats a cuckoo's mouthful, breakfast she'll eat later. After she's finished her morning chores.

Grandpa wants to be left in peace. Grandpa won't go outside so he doesn't need such a mouthful, let that cuckoo hang himself. Grandpa isn't preparing for next year.

Laura will go and spend some time with Rita at Lejasupītes farm, alright? OK? Please, Mīma, please. She'll show Rita her new candy wrappers. One of these is from a candy called *Vāverīte*—that's a squirrel in Latvian—and it's very valuable. It's gilded. It can be exchanged for three *vēžu kakliņi*—crayfish necks—which are not gilded. Fine, OK, fine, Mīma gives her permission to go.

God knows where the kids have wandered off to, but Rita's mama doesn't know. She doesn't know where the kids, those skunks, are hanging out. They take after their fathers, the little parasites.

She doesn't pay attention to Laura any more.

The Lejasupītes farmhouse is similar to Mīma's house. Only here the veranda's windows have been broken.

The large house has been divided into many small flats. At Upītes farmhouse there's only one door that leads to the yard, but here there are many. Each door is in a different color, each obtained from a different place. In Mīma's house there are curtains on every window, here old sheets have been hung, and rags have been stuffed in the broken, open panes. Laura has asked why that's so, but Mīma has responded that she doesn't want to either think or talk about it, why trouble her heart, let people live as they like. It's good that the previous owners of the farmhouse don't see all this, otherwise they'd turn over in their graves in Siberia.

Can one turn over in one's grave? Laura doubts it. Besides that, Mīma doesn't know that people in the graves in Siberia are frozen stiff, because there in the depths of earth there is permafrost. Laura thinks that the owners of Lejasupītes can't after all turn over in their graves. No way they could. But let Mīma think they can.

Rita's mama has cards! She and two other aunties are playing a Latvian card game called Pigs, while chewing on *semushkas*—sunflower seeds—and fighting off flies. Shit-eating flies swarm around the game of Pigs and even more around the real grunting and smelly pigs right there in the farmyard.

Laura can't peel her eyes away.

It's not the aunties that fascinate her, no, not at all. The aunties' armpits and feet stink, Laura doesn't like the Lejasupītes' aunties one bit.

It's the cards. Laura can't take her eyes off the cards.

The last time she saw some cards was in Siberia. In Madalina's hands.

Laura's heart suddenly aches, that's how much she misses Madalina. Madalina with the black curly hair and ever-laughing eyes.

Madalina who was as pretty as the devil. It's just a pity that she didn't have legs.

The legs are with the devil's mother, Jukka, the Finnish guy had said, and had been ready to marry Madalina right on the spot. But she just laughed. The legs that had frozen in the deadly cold were *k chertovoy materi*—with the devil's mother—but nonetheless she was the soul of the Barrack. It was that very Jukka who gave Madalina the nickname Ciganka Moldovanka— the Moldavian Gypsy—because she had cards and she knew how to tell fortunes. Oi, Ciganka Moldovanka!—howled Jukka, sang Jukka, whispered Jukka, cried Jukka, but Madalina just laughed. She had survived because of the cards, just because of the cards. Strong and healthy people had died, but Madalina had not.

"Where is that God's justice?" she yelled, when she got to drink some *samogon*—booze—but no one answered.

Because no one knew where that God's justice was. Madalina continued to earn some money. For her fortune telling she got a bit of milk, some potatoes, sauerkraut, and, now and then, also some lard. Yes, and *samogon*, that too. Even the wife of the *uchastkoviy*—the precinct boss—came to see her. She, who was a comrade. The *uchastkoviy* was a big boss, that's why

Madalina always laid out only good cards for his wife. Just the very best. Cards that showed happiness and wealth, a faithful husband, beautiful and smart children and a climb up the ladder in the upper echelons. The brighter a future Madalina forecast, the more generous the wife of the *uchastkoviy* and other female comrades would be. The comrades came and came, and brought groats and flour. Most of all the women comrades wanted to know about their husbands, that Laura couldn't miss.

Madalina shared with everyone. Madalina without legs, which had frozen totally off in the deadly cold, she was the one who helped the whole Barrack. Not vice versa. Because she had cards.

"Crush my soul, destroy it! Wreck my soul, wreck it, you viper's offspring! Destroy the purity of my heart, destroy it, you dog-faced monsters!" Madalina whispered and crossed herself several times, after she had lied like a horse. It's no honor for a horse, nor for a human being, and the cards have to be asked for forgiveness for the lies, not for the sake of the sack of flour, the bag of sugar, and bread but for the sake of the people of the Barrack. Ciganka Moldovanka was ready to sin a hundred times more and to be boiled in hell's deepest kettle. That's what she said, when Laura was allowed to look on, but when fortunes were told for real, then she couldn't be there.

Back at Lejasupītes farmhouse Manya has tired of the game, and besides—she has to go and check out where her old man has gone. Maybe again dragged himself off to Fredis to get rid of his hangover. Can't hear him sharpening a scythe any more, nor mowing the grass. *Vot*, the bastard, she says. Manya knows quite well how to speak in Latvian.

Dusya doesn't have an old man and she doesn't know Latvian, the *semushkas*—sunflower seeds—are finished and, along with them, finished is her interest in life. The *semushkas* are a passion with her, an obsession, and because of them Dusya will have to go to the kolkhoz's granary to show her tits. For this the White Negro will give her a bit of the kolkhoz's *semushkas*. He can't give too much at one time, for after all it's the property of the kolkhoz, therefore Dusya needs to go there quite often. Just thinking about it makes Dusya laugh.

"It's a pity that no one knows how to tell fortunes," Rita's mama says as she gathers up the worn and greasy cards. I'll have to get a move on," she sighs.

"Laura knows how."

Cards, Laura just wants to hold the cards.

"Put your money where your mouth is." Rita's mama doesn't believe her.

"Them that shits his pants them's gotta wash them." Manya adds and laughs, her big stomach jiggling. Will she have a baby? Laura suddenly feels sorry for that potential child of Manya's.

"This little skunk will tell our fortune! *Etot brat vrag naroda! Nedobitais!*— This midget 'enemy of the people'! Not killed off yet!" Dusya sniggers.

A feeling of being insulted overwhelms Laura as well as anger, yes, which rolls and rises in her like black smoke from hell, because the aunties are laughing at her. Stupid geese, Laura contemplates revenge.

"Laura knows how!"

"Well then lay them out. Who are you going to lay them out for?" Rita's mama asks.

"For Manya."

Laura will lay out the cards just so, lay them out just so!

"Better lay them out for me." Rita's mama throws the cards on the table.

Laura shuffles the cards, they're sticky and not so easy to separate and shuffle. Laura also needs time to push back the black turmoil.

"Well, *davai, davai*, don't drag it out!" Rita's mama won't spend the whole day fooling around with strange children.

"Everyone has to be serious and quiet. You're not allowed to laugh. Cards can't be laughed at and made fun of. Else the cards won't tell the truth. The cards can get angry and then during the night . . ." Laura darkens her voice.

"What at night?" Rita's mama feels some uneasiness. Such a toad, but just look at her talk, and hasn't it been said that now and then from a child's mouth God Himself chooses to say something.

Dusya laughs.

"Shut up!" Rita's mama exclaims.

"*Zatknis, dura gerevennaya*—shut up you stupid country bumpkin!" Maya translates for Dusya.

Laura recognizes the power of cards over people. She remembers how in front of Madalina people used to grow silent. How the desire to know one's future made people shake and tremble as if in front of the greatest power. In front of Madalina, whose legs had frozen off in the deadly cold, the comrade wife of the *uchastkoviy* shivered in her skunk fur coat. Buka's fur coat, Laura's grandmother, which, as luck would have it, had been brought along from Latvia and exchanged for a sack of peas.

Laura brings the cards to the table and applies Madalina's words and delivery.

"Cut the deck in half. Don't whatever you do raise the cards toward you! No!" Laura yells out in horrendous fright, because Rita's mama is ready to do precisely that. Rita's mama draws back her hand. She obeys, obeys Laura! "Pull out four cards."

Rita's mama pulls them out. It's just a joke.

"Now, four more. Just don't look at them! Do you want your eyes to rot away?" Laura screeches. "Place them on top of the first ones," Laura commands.

Manya looks on, Dusya falls silent. In Laura's hand the cards have been fanned out like a peacock's tail.

41

"Well, what is it now?" Rita's mama can't wait, as Laura studies the cards and knits her brow, forming deep wrinkles.

"You can still change your mind if you really want to know. Sometimes it's better not to know," Laura says with empathy, just as Ciganka Moldovanka used to say.

"Of course, I want to hear."

"Your husband will come back." Laura knows that Rita's papa has abandoned them.

"Ah, what did I tell you? Ah, what did I say? No need to tell fortunes for that!" Manya bubbles.

"You can't laugh at the cards! Do you want your tongue to dry up and shrivel?" Laura scares Manya.

"Let him come back, I'll show him! I'll tear out his balls by the roots!" Rita's mama is overjoyed at her husband's predicted return.

"But not to you. Jack of diamonds and the queen of spades. You're not the one. You've got blonde hair." Laura doesn't let Rita's mama be happy too soon.

"Oh my God. To whom then?"

"To the one whose hair is dark. You'll lose everything. You'll follow the wrong path. A new life will begin for you. The old one will end for you with the upper echelons because the queen of spades is saying bad things about you." Laura rattles this off like a handful of beans.

"Wait, wait! Can't you slow down?"

"What's that child saying?" Dusya senses that the business is becoming serious.

"The child isn't saying anything. The cards are talking," Laura answers in Russian.

"Oi, *nyemagu*—I can't—this is too much!" Dusya can't help but laugh at Laura, who's talking in Russian.

Just wait, Dusya, you just wait, soon you won't laugh any more. Laura senses that the women are putty in her hands, just like the cards. The big,

Māra Zālīte

fat women with smelly armpits and feet. Laura senses the power she has. Power is pleasant, it's sweet and exhilarating. It spreads in Laura like a peacock's tail, expands like the dealt cards from the deck in her hand. Who owns the revenge? Laura does!

"Quiet, you old biddies! To whom will my husband return?"

"To Manya!" Laura announces. Laura will forecast this for Manya, take this!

What bullshit are you, small asshole, spouting? I have *svoy*—my own husband!"

What kind of a husband is that? Have you been to the *zagss*—the registry office—with him?" Rita's mama attacks Manya.

"Aha, how did the *zagss* help you? He left despite the *zagss*!" Manya doesn't give up.

"That's not all," Laura interrupts. "The ace of diamonds."

"Ah, *schto*—what's that?" now also Manya wants to know.

"Nobody's telling you your fortune! What does it mean, Laurie?" Rita's mama has never really trusted Manya, now shortly her suspicions will be confirmed.

"By itself it doesn't mean anything. It has to be looked at together with other cards." Laura doesn't hide her great knowledge. "The six of spades!" Laura drags out lengthily what she has to say because she senses that her knowledge is slowly coming to an end.

"What does that mean?"

"The queen of hearts. That's you, and it means that there will be a great misfortune."

"What else now?" Rita's mama moans, she's totally crushed. Laura remembers little Ivars, and she suddenly feels a bit sorry for Rita's mama.

"But you can avoid it," Laura gives her hope.

"How?"

"From this moment on, keep all your thoughts to yourself, don't tell anyone anything, because close to you there's a terribly envious person," Laura warns her.

Rita's mama looks now at Manya, now at Dusya. Manya too looks at Dusya.

"What's that child saying?" Dusya asks worriedly. No one answers.

"If you'll keep quiet, the misfortune will pass you by." Laura adds.

"But the upper echelons? What about that? I won't be sent to Siberia, will I?" Rita's mama worries.

"Don't be afraid, only honest and upright people are sent there. Don't hope and don't feel sad! The jack of spades will want to marry the queen of hearts." She's the mother of her friend, after all.

"Me?"

"Yes, via the upper echelons."

"Dear God, via the office? There's only bosses there! Jack of spades? Who could be that jack of spades? The new agriculturist?"

"*Da ti shot razmechtalas*—you must be dreaming—the new *agronom*?"

"The cards don't say that. But the cards say that Manya will stand in your way. The queen of spades! That's a very evil card."

"*Da*, already tomorrow morning I'll drag *svojevo*—my old man—to the *zagss*—the registry office! But *tvojevo*—yours I wouldn't take even for gold! Ah, and you're what? Ready to cheat on your husband with the new *agronom*?"

Rita's mama has already opened her mouth wide in rage, to finally say what she really thinks of Manya, but at the last minute, she remembers that she shouldn't reveal her thoughts to anyone.

"*Vsjo, da*, idiotic those cards, *da*, screw those cards, you, you louse, a skunk of a kid, stop, *da*, get lost, go to your babushka! *Vsjo! Konec filma*—the film's over!"

"Don't swear at the cards, otherwise you'll burn in hell, in the deepest kettle you'll boil! You'll turn over and over in your grave!" Laura yells at Manya, sensing that Manya is not totally vanquished.

"Dusya." Laura quickly changes direction.

"What—Dusya?" Manya is cross.

Laura thinks. What could Dusya do?

"Dusya is going to steal your husband."

"Shteal??" Dusya asks to make sure.

"What?" Manya's totally on fire now, like a match put to discarded flax waste. "Dusya?"

"See, if that jack were on the right side, then something could miscarry, but when the jack is on the left . . . with the nine of spades on top yet. The outcome is totally certain. Later she'll give him back," Laura comforts her.

Laura wants to finish, because she senses that she has got entangled and in too deep, has lied through her teeth and talked a lot of rot, and hasn't eaten breakfast. Just that cuckoo's mouthful. Laura anticipates her soul's destruction and wreckage.

"The cards no longer want to talk," she announces. "Do you want me to lay out some Solitaire for you?"

Rita's mama doesn't want her to, she's got a lot to think over. But Manya does. How will Dusya steal and how will she give back her husband? Manya also says a couple of vulgar words about Dusya. Dusya doesn't understand anything, because that *sobachiy yazik*—dog's language—she's certainly not going to learn! Besides, she doesn't have any *semushkas*, which could revive her spirit. Just indolent dreams are fluttering around Dusya. How she's going to go to the kolkhoz's granary. How she'll show her tits to the White Negro. How she'll again manage to get some *semushkas*.

"Well, *davai*—go on then!"

"Do you want the short or the long Solitaire? The Chinese Plait or Napoleon's Grave?"

"What kind of a grave?" Manya's never heard of Solitaire, but she's suddenly afraid.

"I can lay out Klondike or the common Solitaire. The common one is the best."

Laura stresses this, because she's afraid that Manya may choose the Chinese Plait, or, worse still, Napoleon's Grave, which is a hard Solitaire and which Laura hasn't managed to learn. Ciganka Maldovanka was teaching her, but didn't manage to get as far as Napoleon's Grave. Madalina went back to her country, and Laura—to hers.

"Laura isn't going to lay out Solitaire for you. The cards are angry with you and I don't have the time now."

Laura throws the cards on the table! After all Laura is a busy person.

Laura wants to get away. She doesn't listen to what Manya calls after her. She's got to run. Has to flee! Save herself! It seems to Laura that her armpits also stink. Laura looks to see if they haven't got just as hairy as Manya's, Dusya's and Rita's mama's. Not yet. But she's got to check again in the evening.

———

Five poems

CHRISTINE DE LUCA

Christine De Luca is one of Scotland's foremost contemporary poets as well as a novelist and translator. She is presently the *makar* (poet laureate) of Edinburgh. She writes in both English and Shetland dialect, a blend of Scots with a strong Norse influence. Her poems have been translated into Italian, Norwegian, Icelandic, Swedish, Danish, Finnish, Latvian, Estonian, Polish, Austrian-German, and Welsh.

Translated from Shetland Scots by the poet.

Lament

You dress yourself up
in your very best, then
let your chiselled features
knock me out.
Why do this to me
on my final day?

Every bend in the road is
a gentle inquiry of my thigh; I'll be
in the ditch if you offer another hill,
that deep rolling over westwards,
softening to its soft powdery browns,
lightening to a gouache of greys.

The wind has dropped. Tonight,
every lake is stencilled,
every inlet inlaid. Wormadale
is glorious; Whiteness, Binnaness,
Kalliness, every one a point of land so near,
bidding me come, step across.

No, I will not disturb a thing.
If I as much as breathe
it will all shatter.
Waas to Watsness is
in thrall ta Foula; rising,
always coming closer.

You take me, over and over;
no fight left in me at all.
This is an undressing, a ravishing.
As I pull myself away
I feel stark naked, bewildered
as that hill ewe, newly-sheared.

A fine heifer was killed and flayed
so they could draw the roads of all the earth
on it, the pilgrim life. Mappa Mundi:
map of the known world; vellum of the heart.

Geographies and histories, we think
we've caught them all in points and lines:
they're out of date before the print is dry,
before a satellite can blink.

But all our blemishes and laughter lines
imprinted on our hearts are well beyond
the terra firma of this world; sentient
bearers of our souls and minds;

goodly hemispheres of love, of longing;
mental maps well beyond the library of
all known worlds, beyond a Mappa Mundi,
more than skin-deep. Forever mystified

we stumble on, like airy plant-gatherers
mapping the Happy Isles, the life-force held
in trembling material selves, happening
upon our lives as they unfold.

Christine De Luca

Imprint

Wherever we are, there's always someone further north.
Only at the pole would a compass twirl round, seek
magnetic certainty.

Wherever we are on this spinning hemisphere
Polaris tracks our staggering steps. She's pinned
to the firmament; a support.

Wherever we are, north is a state of mind
with no slack: earth's stitches taken in,
the top grafted off.

Wherever we are, a scanner would suspect
our identity the way a stick of rock displays
its origin.

Wherever we are, slipped loose like homing pigeons,
there is a path north. Something keeps tugging
that invisible thread.

That line where birds, exhausted, cross
a threshold, winter at their back,
or the joyous din of summer before them.

Where, along the sixtieth parallel,
the resonant voice of the fiddle trembles
on a northern palette. Hanging on in

to three score years is listening for that line,
another season of song. It's pushing
against the door, lifting the latch, taking

the fiddle down and tuning what's left to make
the notes. Fingers reach further, grope gently
the missing string, tempt out the melody.

Christine De Luca

Discontinuity

I could blame the way the sea has smoothed
the stones; the silk of touch; the selecting, leaving/rejecting;
and will the heart be there when I come back?

Or I could blame the ringed plover. He was clear/sure
which way to go: this way now, no looking
over your shoulder. Tide doesn't wait;

see the way the swill of joy has drained.
Dance today. Tomorrow you slip
into eternity.

Or I could blame the hush/silence that fills you
till you're at bursting point with all the words
that could be said but you hold back.

It's what happens when you step
in time, but sense a fault-line trembling
through you: this side or that?

Only the sea can weep and sing at the same time:
shade and light: cobalt, ultramarine and then
the breaking surge on shore—
a temptation, a foamy splutter of white.

———

Ballerina, Ballerina

(novel excerpt)

MARKO SOSIČ

Marko Sosič was born in Trieste in 1958. He
has directed for various Slovenian and Italian
theaters, as well as for television and radio,
and is the author of several books. The narra-
tor of this novel is Ballerina, a young woman
with the cognitive faculties of a child, and
each of its fifteen chapters begins with her
first wetting her bed and thereby greeting
a new day. Drawing comparison to William
Faulkner in its expressionistic depiction of
the main character's interior world, *Ballerina,
Ballerina* is a classic of contemporary
Slovenian literature: a hugely popular explo-
ration of a character whose world is divorced
from what we consider as reality.

*Translated from Slovenian by
Maja Visenjak Limon.*

I'm peeing, now. I can feel I'm peeing. I'm cold. I don't want to open my eyes, I don't want to look at the window. I can hear some footsteps. I know, Mama opens the door. I'm on the bed. I can hear her coming closer. Good morning, Ballerina, she says. We must change, it's a new day today. I know. I know very well it's a new day, because I wet myself, and because it's the morning. Mama is drying me. With a towel. It's rough. It hurts. Then she puts stockings on my feet. I know it's winter.

In the evening when Mama and I are standing by the window, the chestnut tree doesn't have leaves and the birds no longer sleep there. She's putting my stockings on, Mama, caressing my toes. Oh, my beautiful Ballerina, she says, we'll put some ointment on now, every night, on your toes, you know. Otherwise you won't dance anymore. Look, what they're like, they must hurt. And she strokes my toes, my feet.

I'm in the kitchen now. Sitting at the table. Looking at the door. Tata is in the hall, smoking and looking at the yard. The ash falls down. He stands and looks. Mama is breaking bread into a cup of coffee in front of me. I look at the milky coffee, I look at the bits of bread falling into it. I grab a spoon. I slurp. I chew, looking at the hall. Tata is looking at the yard. Then he takes his hat off the hook and puts it on. He looks in the mirror hanging on the wall. It's quiet. No one talks. He doesn't look at me. He steps out into the yard, I see him, he's leaving. To the bar, says Mama. I know he'll be home for lunch. I know I'll grab him by his ear. I'll hold it tight. First, I'll be in the corner, on tiptoes. I'll be tall, then it'll be lunch. And I'll hold his ear so that it hurts, later.

I hear footsteps. A woman is standing in the doorway. She's breathing deeply, quickly. I see Mama turn back. From the stove to the door. The woman doesn't say anything, just breathes. Then she says that Srečko phoned. That his mama was run over and is in hospital.

Mama is looking through the window at the yard. She doesn't always look. Sometimes. Now. The table is laid for lunch. I'm standing in the corner, looking at Mama. I see her shoulders and her hair in a bun. She isn't moving, just looking through the window. Karlo walks into the kitchen now. Mama talks. The neighbor came to tell us that Lucija has been run over. Can you take me to Trieste after lunch?

I listen.

Yes, says Karlo. What's happened?

I don't know. She said Srečko phoned. He said that she's been run over. Karlo sits down at the table. I see Tata is coming. He's in the yard. He stops. He coughs, then comes in.

Lucija has been run over, Mama says. Karlo will take me to Trieste. Ballerina is coming with me.

I stand on tiptoe in the corner. Tata is standing in the door. He doesn't speak. He takes off his coat. His hat. He walks to the window. I know what he's doing. He's looking at the thermometer. It's only ten, he says. Then he takes a pencil from the top of the refrigerator. The pencil is always on top of the refrigerator and he takes it now. He writes something down. Mama says that he writes the temperature on a calendar. Every day. Then he turns on the Grundig to listen to the weather forecast. I know. Everyone is quiet then. Sometimes not, because I sing, but Tata says nothing. He turns off the radio and turns on the lights on the gondola. And then he looks at the gondola. And falls asleep at the table.

He's sitting now. I'm sitting, too. Karlo is looking at me. I know he's been in the woods. Mama says he guards the woods so that they're not cut down. Mama says he also looks after the animals in the woods so that they're not killed.

Mama is changing me. Karlo is also changing. Tata is in the kitchen. He's sleeping with his head on the table, holding his ear with his hand. I see him. From the hall. Mama dresses me, the dress with the butterflies. Then the coat. Let's go and see Aunt Lucija, she says. I look at the butterflies on the dress. Mama buttons up my coat. I can't see the butterflies anymore.

Karlo is driving the car. Mama says it isn't his. It belongs to the state. I don't know the state. I don't know who the state is. It has never been in our kitchen.

I'm sitting near Karlo. Mama is sitting behind me, I know. She put on a gray dress and a scarf on her head. I'm wearing the dress with butterflies. Karlo doesn't say anything. Neither does Mama. Now.

I'm looking at the floor. I'm pressing my coat onto the dress so that the butterflies can't fly off. I see bits of branches. I see leaves. Dry leaves. On the ground.

Then I look through the window. I have my hands on the glass. The road falls steeply down. I see houses running past. People on the road running past. I see them and then I don't see them anymore. They're behind me, I don't know where. Then I see other people, other houses. I'd stand on tiptoe. But I can't. I'd sing. I hear Mama. She's singing now. Just a little. Then she says: Don't be scared, Ballerina. We won't fall . . . All the roads in Trieste are like this . . . We're at the top, they're in Trieste . . .

Then Mama says quickly, Look, look there, can you see the sea . . . Can you see it, Ballerina?

I look. I see. I see a blue field. Like in the morning when Mama comes into the room and the chestnut tree in the yard is full of leaves. Suddenly houses aren't running. People aren't running either.

Karlo says we've arrived and that Lucija lives in that house. I look through the window. They don't see me. No one is looking at me. Karlo opens the door. He takes my hand. Come, Ballerina, he says. I'm standing in front of a tall house. I can't see the roof, there are no chestnut trees, there is no yard. Mama takes my hand. Let's go, Ballerina, she says.

Karlo opens a large door. He says it's made of iron. Let's see first if Srečko is home, he says. We go through the door. Mama is holding my hand. There's no light. I can only see it far away, the light. Then we walk on, toward the light. Karlo knocks on the first door. There is no light here. I see Srečko in the doorway. Suddenly the door is open and Srečko stands in front of us. I look at him. He says nothing. Then he says she died. He cries. We follow him. I look at the room. It's a big room. At one end I see two beds. A window on the other side. High up. You can't see through it. Below the window there is a washbasin, a closet and a chair.

Srečko is sitting on the chair. Karlo, Mama and I are sitting on the bed. Srečko is talking. I look at him and listen.

I told her to put her shoes on. She said she wasn't so stupid as to go in slippers. Mama, I said, those aren't shoes, they're slippers. No, no, she said. You're crazy, you can't even buy bread without getting lost in a square somewhere, you can't even get to Spain. Don't you talk to me. I know what slippers are. And she went. She forgot her bag and money, too. She's only getting some bread, I thought, she can go in her slippers. Then she said that she would come soon and that she would cook some pasta for me. Listen to some music, she said and left. She was crossing the road, they said, and lost a slipper. Then, they said, she turned round to go and get the slipper, but a car came and ran her over. The slippers were still there. I took them and cut them up. She didn't die immediately. When I telephoned, she was still alive. She told me to look after myself and not to leave the gas on because it was expensive and we didn't have money to waste, like others do. And then she died.

Srečko is quiet. Karlo says he will help him, if necessary, and Mama also says something. She says he should come to us if he needs anything. Srečko says nothing. I'm looking at his thin hair, his eyes that are red. His arms are hanging by his side as he sits there. I'm warm. I think of my dress with the butterflies. I feel even warmer. I'm afraid, suddenly, that the butterflies will suffocate. I get up, unbutton my coat, walk to the door, open it and go out, to the iron door, I walk faster, I open it, I walk on. I hear Karlo calling me. I walk on. People walk past me, now they look at me. I know they're looking at my butterflies. I don't want them to look at them. I want to be in the kitchen, in the corner, on my tiptoes, looking at the yard through the window. I want to sing. Karlo grabs my hand. Slowly, slowly, Ballerina, he says. Mama is here, too. You'll catch a cold, she says and buttons up my coat and the butterflies on my dress are covered again.

Again, houses are running past and people. Mama says I mustn't catch a cold because when I have a cold I don't sleep at night and I can't dream. That I break things then, if I don't sleep, that I pull everything out of the closet and throw it out into the yard and they have to shut me in the pantry then, even at night, like they did with grandad Nono, who is now in heaven. They shut him in the pantry, too, says Mama. I mustn't catch a cold. And if you don't calm down in the pantry, you have to go to Elizabeta's because I get so tired, Mama says. And if I can't stay at Elizabeta's those gentlemen in the car come and take me to hospital, Mama says. I know that. I see them. They stop in the door and smile. Then I go with them. And then, when they bring me back, Mama sings, I know she sings, because I can hear her, even there, where they take me. I hear her voice and I think she's there somewhere in the hall or the pantry, singing. Mama shuts herself in the pantry when they take me away, I know. I can see her shutting herself in there. I look into the kitchen from the yard and I see her. First she cries. When I'm shut away, I hear her sing, too.

Now it's evening. Mama and I are standing by the window. Mama says I should look at the stars, I should find my own star and give it a name. Then she talks. Poor Lucija, she says . . . She experienced so little good, always in that hole with no windows. Watching the door, all her life. Seeing who came and who left, taking in mail for the other people in the building and that's how it went. Silvester was nice. He played the organ in the church. Poor Srečko. What will happen to him, eh? What do you say, my beautiful Ballerina? And she takes me to bed. It's dark. I listen to her footsteps. They're moving away. Now I know my mama is in her room and that Tata is already asleep.

· · · · ·

The postman says there is no good in the world since they went to the moon years ago with Sputnik. He says the stars will take revenge and that things will be worse and worse in the world. As he says this, he puts a telegram on the table. I'm standing in the kitchen, looking at him. Tata is standing, too, looking through the window toward the yard as if he can't see the postman. The postman is standing in the door, looking at the telegram he's put on the table. Mama is looking at it, too. I'm looking at the postman. Mama doesn't get a glass, she doesn't pour him a drink. I'm standing in the corner, watching. I'm wearing a gray shirt and a blue skirt. Mama says that I got the skirt for my twenty-fifth birthday, Mama says I'm thirty now and that time goes quickly. She tells me this when she dresses me, after she has washed me and combed my hair in the hall in front of the mirror. I see everyone is looking at the telegram on the table. The postman said so. I've brought a telegram from Australia, he said and put it on the table. And then he talked about the moon and how there will be no good in the world. Tata is still looking through the window. He's smoking now, too, and shaking the ash onto the floor. Then Mama sweeps. Always, when Tata shakes the ash on the floor. I think Tata is looking at the sky, I think that he is quietly talking to Uncle Feliks, like Karlo. I think he wants to go to Uncle Feliks. The postman is still in the doorway. Then Mama picks up the telegram and says:

Here, Franc!

Tata takes the telegram and opens it. He looks at the postman and opens it. The postman is still standing in the door. Then Tata says:

Albert is coming, next week. Mama's eyes light up. I see.

Is he coming with his wife? asks the postman.

Tata looks at him. Tata is looking at the postman in the doorway and doesn't say anything. Mama pours a glass. The postman drinks it, opens his mouth. We watch him. Mama sometimes says that she never knows if the postman will ever start breathing again after he has had a drink. Then he breathes. Always. He breathes, smiles and leaves.

Marko Sosič

Tata sits down. He looks at the gondola, sitting with the telegram in his hand. I'm still in the corner, looking at him.

I'm sitting at the table, eating pasta.

It's good, the pasta, isn't it, Ballerina? says Tata. I look at him. I know my mouth is full and the sauce is running down my chin. I know, I don't feel, because Mama gave me the drops earlier, to make me calm, I saw her. I know I don't feel. Tata is looking at his plate. Then I see there are others around the table, we're all here and I think it's my birthday. Josipina, Karlo, Tata, Mama, everybody is here. I look at them. Then I put down my fork with pasta on it and I hold his ear, Franc's, my father's. He doesn't say anything. He lets me pull his ear and he keeps looking at his plate with pasta. Then I take Karlo's hand and pinch him. First he moves it away, then lets me pinch him. I watch Josipina. Now I'm watching her and holding a fork. No one says anything. Not even Mama, who is standing behind me and eating pasta from a small pan. I see her. Mama likes pasta. Sometimes she says: Oooh, it's so good. And I watch Josipina. She looks like Mama. Her eyes are like Mama's, like Elizabeta's. Josipina, my sister.

She talks quietly. Mama says she talks like a sparrow, like the birds sleeping in the tree top when it's night. And sometimes when I lie and look from my bed at the window, with the chestnut tree outside, I think Josipina is up there with the birds sleeping in the tree.

And I watch her. She smiles and slowly picks up some pasta. Mama says Josipina is educated, that she's a teacher, but Giacomino said she should stay at home and look after the children. Poor Josipina, Mama says sometimes as we stand by the window, looking at the place where Mama had the best day in her life. The first day they were married, Giacomino hit her. Josipina cried, says Mama, because she was happy to have married Giacomino, but he didn't know she was crying because she was happy, and he hit her. Poor Josipina, says Mama, she's never cried since. And I watch her. I think I haven't seen her for a long time, only once when Karlo took me to her, because Mama was tired and Elizabeta was ill. I know Karlo took me to her. I see her small apartment, I see Giacomino lying on the bed without clothes, reading a book. I hear Josipina tell me how he has read that book a few times already, then I hear her tell him to get dressed, then I see him get up from the bed and I see something dangling between his legs until he puts his pants on. Then I'm there, I know, in her kitchen and her children are with me, two boys. Mama says they're the same age as me, that they're my nephews and that they never come to visit. Mama says she's their *nona* and it would be nice if my nephews sometimes came for a visit.

Then I know I'm alone, that Giacomino who shoots at planes at night isn't there, that Josipina isn't there because she said she was going to iron a few things at the watchmaker's. And I'm alone with my two nephews. And I hear them say to me to come to their room and lie on the bed. I go to their room and I lie on the bed and my nephews lie next to me and they caress me. I know, they are caressing me on my face and then they caress my arms and then legs and I know my ears are ringing, that I'd like to say something, that I'd like to tell them something and I'd like to stand on tiptoe and sing and I'd like to hear Mama sing with me, and I'd like to be with Ivan, who is somewhere far away and going to school so that he can cure me, and I see the field, I suddenly see it full of weeds, I see my two nephews in the field, tramping it down and laughing and saying that there will never be any more potatoes in the field, that weeds will grow and that the field won't be able to breathe. And then I see rain falling on the field, on the weeds and on the nephews, who are laughing and saying that the weeds will grow even more because the sun will come out after the rain and it'll be warm and the weeds will grow even more, the weeds on the field, and then I sing, loud, loud . . .

Ciao, ciao, bambina! Un bacio ancor
e poi per sempre ti perderò . . .

And then I'm no longer at Josipina's. Then I'm home, like now in the kitchen and I'm just looking at her, at Josipina, picking up pasta with her fork.

Suddenly Mama says, Albert is coming from Australia.

He's coming with his *signorina*, says Tata, smiling. Mama says we must give him a good welcome, that he hasn't been home for twenty-five years and that we must forget everything. What happened, happened, says Mama and starts clearing the plates. I'm sitting at the table, listening. And Karlo says that he won't look at a whore in our house who went with the whole American barracks, that he doesn't give a shit if Albert fell in love with her.

I don't know what a whore is, I don't know what a whole American barracks is, I don't know what shit is and I don't know what it means that Albert fell in love with her. I feel warmth on my face, I'd like to get up and stand on tiptoe in the corner and look through the window at the yard.

Then Tata also says what happened, happened. Josipina's eyes are sparkling.

Mama says that Albert and Josipina loved each other very much and that she was very sad when he went to Australia. I watch Karlo. He drinks a glass of wine and looks at his plate.

After all, says Tata, if you have a job, it's because Albert went to Australia! Then Karlo lifts his eyes and also says: Well, what happened, happened. Now

65

I want to get up, I want to push him into the yard, Karlo. Let him go to the woods, let him work, let him buy the paint so that we can paint the house. I feel Mama's hands on my shoulders. It's alright, it's alright, Ballerina. You'll see Albert and then it'll all be alright, she says. Then I stop thinking that I want to push Karlo into the yard and Tata says that the room needs to be prepared. That Albert and his *signorina* will sleep in the room Mama and he sleep in and that they will come to my room. We'll sleep with Ballerina, says Tata and looks at the gondola that always stands on the television that's called Telefunken. Then he says: Turn on the television, let's watch the news.

Josipina turns on the television and we watch the *telegiornale*.

Now it's evening. Mama and I are standing by the window and she says it's summer, the windows should stay open so that I can hear the crickets. Then she says: I'm really happy that Albert is coming, and she walks me to my bed. And then she leaves and closes the door. I lie there, listening to the crickets. I know I'm going to fall asleep soon.

Tata has gone to the barber's, says Mama, because Albert from Australia is coming today. She's combing my hair. She has dressed me in a pink dress with a bow, the one I wore for my birthday, once in the past. I know that that was then. Ivan was still here and said to me, Happy Birthday, Ballerina, and he gave me a bunch of flowers. I looked down at him because he was little and his ears stuck out.

Mama's hair is nicely combed, too, and she's wearing her party dress with the nice, starched collar. Karlo went to Venice airport with his car that isn't his. Mama said that Karlo is going to pick up Albert at the airport, when I stood at the window and everything was blue, even the yard was blue as I watched Karlo leave.

They'll be here any moment now, says Mama, looking through the window at the yard. I'm standing by the door, looking at her. She's looking through the window, walking up and down, up and down. Then she says: Josipina is here . . .

I see her. She's crossing the yard, coming into the hall, then the kitchen.

Srečko is coming, too, says Mama to Josipina.

Good, says Josipina, taking her shoes off. She say's they're too tight because they're new. I look at her. She's sitting at the table, rubbing her toes.

Then Mama says Srečko is here, too. I don't know if it is him, I don't know if this is Srečko, my cousin, like Mama says, because his mama was Lucija, the sister of Franc, who is my Tata.

In the evening, as we are standing by the window before it is night, Mama says that she hasn't seen him for a long time, Srečko, only Karlo sometimes meets up with him and then comes home drunk, Mama says. She's looking at the field, at the cherry tree, and she says: He must have aged, Srečko . . .

Mama says that when a person gets old like she has, they soon go to heaven.

I hope he doesn't get lost, says Mama then and puts me to bed.

Now Srečko is in the kitchen. Mama steps closer to him. I see her. She goes to him, puts her arms around him and then strokes his thin hair. He smiles. I see he has very few teeth.

Allora, our Australian's coming, he says, nodding.

Mama smiles. I see she's happy. When Mama is happy, I'm not scared. Everyone is happy because Albert is coming, even Josipina, even Karlo and Tata, who's still at the barber's.

Mama says that Albert and Srečko are very fond of each other. That they used to fish together in the pond, they rode bicycles together and wherever one went, the other followed.

How time passes, eh, Srečko, she says and looks through the window at the yard.

Now Tata is coming. We all see him through the window. He's in the yard. He stops. I see the back of his neck and the straw hat. You can see his hair has been cut, you see it under his hat, on the back of his neck. When Tata's hair has been cut, I feel as if I want to cry, I want to sob, because he looks like a little boy, like Ivan when he goes to school or when they cut his hair for the holidays. We must look nice on holidays, says Mama, and today is a holiday, and she goes out into the yard where Tata is.

We're all in the yard.

We're standing under the chestnut tree, in which birds sleep at night, looking at the gap where, Mama says, Karlo will bring Albert. It's nice in the shade, says Srečko, wiping his forehead. I see his hand, how it trembles. He wipes his forehead with a trembling hand and says: Oh, they should be back from Venice by now.

And we all look in the direction Karlo, Albert and his *signorina* should come. I don't know. I've never seen his *signorina*, she hasn't been in our kitchen yet so that I could see her.

Mama says she had long red hair, that she was very beautiful and that she's called Ida. She told me this once by the window as she looked toward Mount Čaven and Angel Mountain, which is hers and hers only, she says.

I hear a car. The others hear it too. I see. Tata takes a step forward, adjusts his hat, Mama adjusts her skirt, Josipina wipes the dust off her shoes and Srečko once more wipes his forehead. I see his eyes are sparkling, Srečko's.

The car is here. Albert, my brother steps out, Ida, his *signorina*, follows him. They both have a lot of dry leaves on their clothes because in the car driven by Karlo there's always a lot of dry leaves. I know this from when he drives me to Elizabeta's and he opens the window and the leaves twirl around me. Karlo says: It's draughty. I'll close the window.

Karlo is smiling. So are Albert and Ida. They walk toward us. They are coming closer. Now they are here. Tata hugs Albert. They hold on to each other firmly. Tata cries. Then he isn't crying any more. Then Albert goes to Mama and kisses her. He caresses her gray hair and her face and holds her hands. And then he kisses Josipina, hugs Srečko and me. Hello, Ballerina, he says. Ida is there, the *signorina*. I see her. She's standing at a distance, smiling. In the evening Mama will tell me that she was embarrassed, poor Ida. In the evening, when Mama sleeps in my room and Tata is in my room, too. Then I see Mama step over to Ida and shake her hand. Tata does the same, as do Josipina and Srečko.

Now we're in the kitchen. I'm looking at Albert, my brother from Australia. He has beautiful eyes, Albert, like the sea, says Mama. Ida has similar eyes. Mama says that people who love each other always have something in common on their faces.

Albert and Ida are handing out parcels. One for everyone. Mama says that they are presents and we must open them. I see Tata has already opened his. Mama says it's an ashtray in the shape of Australia. Oooh, how beautiful it is, she says. Then Karlo unwraps his present. Mama says he got a bottle with photographs of kangaroos. It's Josipina's turn. She unwraps it slowly. Then she says: Oooh, what a beautiful plate! and she shows us it. I see Josipina holding the plate. Then I hear Albert say that a photograph of the capital of Australia is stuck on the plate. Everyone says once more: Oooh, how nice it is. Then Srečko unwraps his present. Albert says that it's a barrel organ, where you have to turn the handle and then music plays. Albert says that it plays the song *Lili Marleen*. Then Mama says I should unwrap my present. I can't. She helps me. I see her hands untie the ribbon and remove the paper, then I see a box, I see Mama opening it and then everyone says: Oooh! Look how beautiful it is, says Mama and tells me I got a dancer, a ballerina, like me, only I don't have a short, lacy skirt, Mama says and turns something on the box the dancer is standing on, Ballerina, me. Then Ballerina twirls and moves her legs, up, down, up, down. Then Mama opens her present. And again everyone says: Oooh! What a beautiful headscarf, thank you, Albert, thank you, Ida, says Mama and puts the headscarf back in the paper. I'm standing in the corner now. Looking at them. Albert and Ida. And the others. They're drinking, eating and talking. Albert is talking about wooden houses. He says that he builds small wooden houses, that the deserts in Australia are big and there are many fires. Then he says he will stay a month, visit his friends, and then go back. Then they go on drinking. I see Mama. She's looking at Albert's face and listening. I see she's happy and I'm not afraid of anything. I haven't had my drops and I'm not afraid. I'm holding Ballerina in my hands and listening. Srečko is talking now. He says he will go to Vienna, to visit Beethoven's grave, because Beethoven has been in heaven for a long time, Mama says. Then they pour wine for Srečko. Karlo pours it and Srečko is talking and talking and everyone is laughing and then Srečko sings some music written by Beethoven, he tells us, and then he cries and everyone keeps laughing, like they always do when Srečko is talking about Beethoven and crying and the others laugh. I look at Ida. She's looking at Mama. Mama doesn't see that Ida is looking at her, Mama is also laughing because everyone is laughing and if it's a holiday, she always says, everybody needs to be happy.

Then I see Karlo go to the pantry. I know he'll come back with the accordion. He's already here, sitting, pulling the bellows, as Tata says. And then Karlo plays and Albert dances with Mama and Tata dances with Ida and then I want to stand on tiptoe, look at the yard and sing. My ears are ringing, I'm standing on tiptoe, singing.

Ciao, ciao, bambinaaaaaa!
Un bacio ancooor . . .

Then Karlo is no longer playing the accordion. I see Mama quickly go to the pantry. I know she'll give me the drops. I pick up the plate that Josipina was given as a present and throw it at the door. Oooh, everyone says and Mama comes back from the pantry and gives me the drops.

I see Albert and Ida looking at me. Everyone is looking at me, then they smile and Mama picks up the bits of the plate with the capital of Australia on it. I'll glue it together, says Josipina and smiles. Then Srečko picks up the barrel organ and turns the handle so that the song *Lili Marleen* is played.

La la, la la la la, la la, la la la la . . .

And he sings quietly and turns the handle. Then he smiles and everyone claps.

———

Marko Sosič

Orpheus in the Underworld 1999 (Dead Times)

(poem)

VINCENZO BAGNOLI

Italian poet Vincenzo Bagnoli was born in 1967. Following his PhD in Italian literature from the Ca' Foscari University of Venice, he worked as a research assistant for several years, publishing monographs and essays on Italian literature. Vincenzo co-founded the literary magazine *Versodove: Rivista di letteratura*. He has published three volumes of poems, with work appearing in top Italian poetry magazines, newspapers, and blogs. He has also played in a postpunk band and contributed to several documentary films.

The following poem, in six breathtaking movements, also appears in *Offscapes*, a beautiful bilingual (Italian-English) book-length collaboration with translator/photographer Valeria Reggi, exploring Italian industrial decay.

Translated from Italian by Valeria Reggi.

’Αθεΐας ωδή *"So this is permanence, so evenings die"*
in 6 movements, all *allegri*
                    Temps passés Trépassés Les dieux qui me
                    formâtes Je ne vis que passant ainsi que vous passâtes

I mov.: Dante's Metamorphoses

betamethasone disodium phosphate
zero and six-hundred fifty-eight
2-mercaptoethanesulfonate
terfenadine and ketoconazole
electrocardiograph abnormalities
                    (and ask me whether I hate promises):
this is the formula for good breathing,
but few other words remain
and the wound of the voice lies
within the warm limbs
the softness of sinuses and turbinates,
of the omohyoid and the hyoglossus.
The lip is torn and the above and the below
are no longer together,
but not laughter, rather the sneering
of the *homme qui rit*, something cruel
or the stupor of aphasic apnea:
and not the ecstasy of anaesthesia,
but the stupefaction of mucous membranes
worn out by winds, broken into clods,
an adam's mud now sterile.
(You know I have difficulty hearing

your voices, followed for what . . .
what are you looking for in these fissures?
all the roads leading inside are blocked
and inside there's nothing to find:
only the fluids that filled me,
like wax in an empty mould . . .)

While discomfort remains on the surface,
the satan of flabby comebacks
behind the curtain of the soft palate
leads all the buzzing swarms
of silly scrappy hisses in the ears;
the sphenoid sinus, the infundibulum of suffering,
of aching at the base of the brain,
the stooge of the hypophysis,
also seriously damaged,
sends remorse, pains in the ass,
intense twinges (and an ice-cream
or a cold proposal are enough to relieve it).
The best part is hyperosmia
but an attorney defends the case
of other gags, of dysphasia,
endocrinous dereistic psychosis;
the doigt savant, like a scratching chicken,
searches for guilt and spreads disaster:
the only remedy is baptism
in chlorine, lithium and cortical joys,
lavished along dark internal canals:
who knows which locks adjust
the high and low tides of moods,
perhaps the ostiomeatal obstruction . . .

II mov.: Gulf Stream

Faults, failures, clots, jams,
marmalades of junctions and membranes,
there are always roadworks
blocking traffic and the flow,
something inside is always upside down:
the fatigue of the intertransversarii,
labours of serratus anterior and triceps surae,
rashes not in the handbooks
sepsis in ambush behind the atlas.
So in the design, in the forma urbis,
there are the areas that began
to work little by little
in their own way, or not to work;
against all expectations and programs
in strange directions they develop
the bitter luxuriance that stirs within,
the sedition, a hidden rhythm
of cells inflamed, reluctant
not rebel, but rather inclined
just to mind their own business . . .

(only a swirl in the stream
such a small thing seen from above
even so at the end the total isn't right).
Urban tissue pathologies
or those sentences already written
in gloomy chromosome seventeen
                    (and ask me whether I hate promises).
Accidents never happen you should know:
not even the bite of Treitz's muscle,
anxiety, tumultus sermonis, anthraxes,
or pervigilium veneris *solo*,
perversion, moral dementia,
impatient jungle proliferation
(Old Faithful Koch Bacillus),
equinoctial burning of whines,
kind tabes of adolescence,

afternoon marsh fevers,
makes you an idiot for life,
inflammatory process emotion
continues after the dream in the street . . .
Leprosy, tangled filariae
imitate bowels and seminal ducts;
Fate writes sentences on the bones,
hysterical conversion, toxins,
paralogies from the depths of the sea
at the base of the brain polyps, hippocampi.
Which is the innocent species of this
monkey unleashed without reason,
the rhythmic hard core of histamine?
All the science of euergetes,
the beautiful panorama of institutes,
of schermographies and tomographies
can only eviscerate you more than pain,
solve with steel the uncertainties,
of anal-vulvar deformities:
to balance with damage, to suggest
the bloody shortening of the limb
                    (and ask me whether I hate promises),
and torment imperfection a little,
the sad twin of your little heart:
the small, blind, dumb animal,
the bat in too little light,
the line in the ultra-violet spectrum,
the obtuse triceratops moving forward
head down, striking the belly.

III mov.: 'αιτίαι (Das Stockholm Krematorium)

And then, at the end, what? Darkness, death,
ashes: nothing to fear, then . . .
but here we end up as dust long before that,
as very fine, thin filings,
specs of dust flying all around:

the scales of a snake skin,
the *this is the end*, the squeaks of fear,
the signatures on the contracts, the "I am busy",
packaged and mortgaged time
as if it were already ours,
the waiting of all those cigarettes
the delightful jokcs of calcium and carbon
(the *other than I am* is already undone after seven years:
anything but *solve* and *resurrectio carum*)
lucid consternation for the past
                              (and ask me whether I hate promises).
The longer evenings, almost without shadows,
our tales as pounds of flesh
bitten by wheels or melted over years
by the bitter acid of time,
fear in the veins which kills,
glass angel with diamond smile,
sharp cutting steps over our sighs,
looks, thoughts, words and voices
fixated in the crystal of glasses:
the night slips by addicted to
the dream of ending too soon,
lifeless are the plaster faces solidified
in the damp, apathetic, bitter light
of this conditioned reflex
of these discrete lives: the I, the stubborn
eternal desert of repetition:
throw forward the name, headlong,
stick it into the belly at every turn
of the hungriest and most merciless days
and say I, I, yet again,
with the short breath of a dog trying

Vincenzo Bagnoli

to speak but the voice doesn't come out,
and reaffirm it once again in writing
with one's own expression of consensus
undersigned several so many times, my name
is poured into waters hot and cold
by the angelic Temperance of databases,
corals in which I will collapse,
I cell, animula or blastula:
plasma transfused into recent veins,
from behind enemy lines in Udine or Ellis
Island, from Sidi Barrani, from Omaha Beach,
always trying to make it last
without shedding a drop: this is what
excites the organs of life,
certainly not the erotic arcadia
of the *bon sauvage* unbound in the cellar,
nor a small boy's tiny erection,
the German E flat of the I,
nor the haloed hard-on in heaven,
the omnipotence of divine love
(the infinite reduced to poodles)
or the cry of ferocious amerika.

IV mov.: Pistis Sophia

Eternity are the chronic encounters
which find us at every crossroads,
eyes mirrored in car windows,
the small change, the anniversaries:
trembling waves of various existences,
rather than rolling breakers of great emotions,
leaden conspiracy of sky and seconds:
possessions abandoned in drawers,

the grey personal archaeologies,
identical in cycles and manias,

complaints always new with variations,
repetition, compulsory identities
within the folds of this oblique zone
written by the twisted diagonals
of all the lines of the external walls:
life Abolished from without . . .
Magnetic skies of sidelong glances
seem to give bitter advice
sometimes met even otherwise,
suspended in the dark, images at the end
of alleys, a gloomy shivering:

and we cling to a fear
in order to overcome and carry on
with our bones and so much rubbish
to appear then to somebody else
in the evening, in the dark, at the end of an alley,
This, the dull horror of Mr. Anywhere
                    (and ask me whether I hate promises).

The small world is held together
by the scaffolding of transport timetables,
their connections and their routes
precise in their details, the omniscience
of satellite networks, of media:

Vincenzo Bagnoli

it doesn't need a catastrophe, it takes very little,
a small human error or even less
to unroll kilometres into metres
to bring back the ancient fury
of the submultiple in steps and seconds
(and ask me whether I hate promises).

Little is left of all that was built:
only the permanent building site, the style,
(I don't mean the products, now only
flattened drink cans, single-dose sachets of ketchup,
outlive glacial erosion).
The sense of making is over,
only squalid leftovers remain:
excavated soil, broken pylons,
poles in the mud, metal cages,
broken wire netting, metal sheets and fences,
splintered wood and wet sand,
Chernobyl, Mostar, My Lai, Bhopal:
behind the eloquence and persuasive words
there lie the bare beams of trade
                    (promises, I've had enough of them now).

V mov.: The Moons of Saturn (Saturnalia)

Three little girls grew tired
in Balashikha but not the short-sighted
omnipotence of the conservative
former minister freely promising
happiness to everyone,
even to billions of Chinese and Indians
(then he dies like a dog like everyone else):
the same promise made to a handful of Jews
(all of them dead and buried generation after generation)
by a god counting minutes and money.
If ever there were such a god, he would deserve
to be dead, extinguished not in embers,
but in ashes, consumed and fallen upon
the shoulders of righteous people.

Under an iron sky of uniform clouds
with the colour of a hostile glance
(no Ovid ever saw any like this)
what is permanence, the memory
of wrongdoing, the justice of history,
the mockery of an exile's lament?
and what value do you read in the landscape,
the eye distracted, the step oblique,
tense, *crispé*, crouched up, stooping,
halted on the verge of change
on the brink of horizons dark and livid
like a burnished steel blade?
a sordid thrill of eternities
torn to pieces, a rotten garden
mud feeding diseased roots:
will this ruin then generate summer?
the Feasts of March cry on the windowpanes
and chill the eyes,
raindrops on the sea, poison
in the wind on the irises, geraniums,
in a chameleon garden,
toad hedges at the far end of the room,
slimy horror, morbid cadence.

Vincenzo Bagnoli

Under a white sky slave to disillusion,
in a landscape of ice and silence,
a snow flake floated down slowly:
erratic torment, sweet grace,
this is the day I always wait for,
a spiral transforming every substance,
a spark, a Siberian whirlwind,
static deformation of the air,
a sudden mechanical apocalypse.
This is the time of the day when we die
and then we live again in bodies
made through silent alchemy
with ashes and methane, snow and mud,
in the chill of colours on the horizon;
it's the time of the day without words
without a name for its secret,
or to say where it happens:
these are the painful truths of sunrise,
the steep races of half-sleep;
the dream of tainted twilights
falls from the obscure peaks of the cosmos.

Under a barred sky of nameless anthracite,
auto-da-fé of gigantic nothing,
all the knights of Scorpio,
poisoning the years and the days,
come from Rigel's splendour:
seven stars of prey in a crown
and fear with trembling arms
tears up the street of fast screams,
dragging the wakes of screeching silence;
death is lying in wait in the grim,
ferocious November midnights,
shiny and sparkling with frost,
with a hundred faces hatred comes forth
and all equally made of stone:
infantile shivers are not enough,
to keep them at bay.

Under a sky of cooled lava and dead suns,
between faraway blood-red barriers,
screaming anxieties in clear silence,
in the agony of remote space,
force fields scattered and shaken,
sprinkled with infertile lapilli,
life dries off in a serir of bones

and while passing by you feel the harshness
of what has no more voice or time,
if not in stone, the soil of the dead.
Along the road the tarmac cracks,
the livid entropy wounds the walls,
throws the debris into the muddy bottom
of the liquid shipwrecks of the gaze,
water in the lungs, numerator,
blue marbled dreams, Morse code:
the crazy, blinded anguish smiles
from the dim landscape of the rooftops,
a glass smile crept into the heart
removing calendar shreds,
the speeches of the stars, the embodied
total map of destruction.

Vincenzo Bagnoli

VI mov.: Ha Daisu

None of this is real (is it?)
Not the stupid death sowed
in the suburban edge through negligence.
Not even the white smoke between rooftops,
the same colour as the plaster sky
that tore flesh off our bones.
History also passed nearby so try
looking for traces, but everything
is a wide farrago, incoherent sands,
and you have to climb up deposits
of facts of no importance,
dull minutes of worthless lives,
rewinding metres of virgin tape,
of empty space, blank tape or blank verse,
white noise (it didn't record anything,
something must have gone wrong),
delays, then interpret the mistakes
of the ticket machine,
crash into the confused cabalas
of useless days, of pocket money,
receipts, notes and clippings,
signatures, labels, brands, reputation:
my name is part of the landscape
and I am this name and this body,
the character adapted to the sound,
the sketch in a revue, a catchphrase.
I am here, not anywhere else: a glance,
the ten-millionth interval
of longitude between the parallels,
the gap between cobblestones,
the space between stretched out ribs,
a broken cage (what animal was it before?
you can't tell the remains calcined
from porphyry pavement cemented with tarmac).
If even the cage of the meridians
crumbles and they are in freefall,
in this jerky, oblique movement,

let years come and go, darkly,
a quiet tide brushing the earth:
we will go to the grave, we will
go down the whirl well-seasoned in flavours,
artificial and natural yeasts,
tanned by acids and blows,
carefully eviscerated and hollowed out.
Do you remember every step after
the end of some job interview,
their colour, the aged evening,
you, aged too and taken farther away?
Not really away, always going back home,
and this, my bitter spending time
recants at every step and, in the end, laughs at it
in the courtyards of Bologna.

———

Vincenzo Bagnoli

The day I learned to fly

(novel excerpt)

STEFANIE KREMSER

Stefanie Kremser was born in Duesseldorf, Germany, in 1967, and grew up in São Paulo, Brazil. She studied documentary film at the University of Television and Film in Munich and lives with her husband, the Catalan writer Jordi Puntí, in Barcelona.

    The day I learned to fly is her third novel (first published in Germany as *Der Tag, an dem ich fliegen lernte* in 2014). Luisa's life is saved by an Englishman just after birth, which leads her, later in life, to delve into the past of her own family, in both a small Bavarian town and Brazil. In compellingly beautiful prose with unexpected turns, Kremser fabulates the strange consequences of emigration, the drive to unearth one's origins, and the legacy of family legends. The excerpt here is chapter 1 of this novel, which does not yet have an English-language publisher.

Translated from German by the author, with the help of Julie Wark.

La-le-lu, nur der Mann im Mond schaut zu, wenn
die kleinen Babies schlafen, drum schlaf auch du.
Lo-lee-lu, only the man in the moon's watching when
the little babies sleep, so you shall sleep, too.
—GERMAN LULLABY BY HANS GAZE

My mother, who has freckles and lives under the Milky Way: this is Aza. At night I whispered her name without being able to call her mother, or mum, or mummy, and the more I repeated it, the more I believed I understood its meaning. Aza, she who has wings. Aza, who must have thought I was a bird and perhaps hoped that one day I'd fly to that place to which she'd been drawn. Aza, who was wrong but somehow proved right in the end. I missed her even before I was separated from the umbilical cord, before I could have imagined what awaited me just four hours after I was born, in a single room of the Red Cross clinic in Taxistrasse, West Munich.

Aza rose from the bed with a painful groan, slid her toes into her flip-flops and lifted me out of the bassinet. It was the first time she touched me. It was the first time she looked at me. She hadn't wanted to see me before that. She hadn't wanted to see anyone, closing her eyes as soon as she heard footsteps approaching. She lay still when someone put a hand on her arm or when something moved behind her, even if it was only the harmless curtains fluttering in the scent of a storm. When Nurse Marianne wheeled me into the room with her squeaky soles the only thing Aza wanted was to keep facing the wall, staring at the grains of the wallpaper. She felt the pattern with her fingertips, groping her way through teardrop-shaped obstacles and seeing in the twists and turns a distant land of valleys and rivers.

Now she was almost tender as she picked me up and held me close but gingerly as if I was a cluster of fresh-laid eggs her parents had sent her out to gather in the chicken run. With me in her arms, she carefully sat on the window ledge and slowly swung her legs outside. She exhaled pain in ragged breaths and beads of sweat dripping from her forehead. The view over the rooftops of Neuhausen was rain-coloured. Sunbeams nudged through retreating leaden clouds, polishing up roofs and treetops. Everything smelled of earth and bark. Starlings chirruped, somewhere a dog was barking, and a cyclist whizzed through puddles on the newly washed cobblestones. Otherwise it was quiet. But then my stomach started to rumble and, gulping in a great mouthful of air, I let it out in a screech, which turned into yelling, first demanding, then angry, and with each gasp I jerked my body around like a fish snapping for air. I opened my purple mouth wide, screamed, and clenched my fists until they lost all colour, becoming bloodless and almost translucent. Aza stretched out her arms, holding me, this bawling red-faced infant fury away from her, out towards the tower of the Dom Pedro Church. It was 7 September 1994, Wednesday afternoon, six o'clock and, when the church bells began to ring, Aza rocked me to the rhythm of the independence anthem which Emperor Dom Pedro I had once composed for her country: "and freedom dawns on the horizon of Brazil, *já raiou a liberdade no horizonte do Brasil*." Just then, her left rubber thong, now free from her toes, fell five stories down into the bushes of the narrow strip of garden skirting the hospital. It glowed like a fat flower among the dark leaves of an elderberry bush, and Aza was still holding me in outstretched arms, now weak and trembling with the effort. Starlings chirruped, somewhere a dog was barking, footsteps echoed in the street; Nurse Marianne stood in the doorway and her shriek tumbled down, down, down, sounding all the way to the street. Then my mother made her decision.

I fell, following in the wake of the yellow thong. I, too, was a little yellow, around my nose. Since I had no past I couldn't have seen my life flash before my eyes, but what I could glimpse for a second was the future: the lush green of late summer chestnut leaves fading out to become a jungle thicket, a darker, blurry, unfathomable tangle of tropical forest, and I had a whiff of orchids that smelled like elderflower as a large pair of warm hands pulled me out of the air into a wide arc, slowing me down like a pendulum and rocking me, as gently as they could, to rest.

Fergus, the recently arrived rugby player from Greenwich, pressed me tight to his chest and fell to his knees. He began to tremble. That was better than any up-and-under he'd ever caught in his career as a Southeast London fullback, but only the sniffing dog of his girlfriend, with whom he'd moved in only a few days earlier, was there to witness the amazing feat.

"What on Earth?" asked Fergus, looking up at the sky searching for an answer, more or less around the fifth floor where an appalled Nurse Marianne was leaning out of the window. Four months later he became my godfather, my godlike all-protecting saviour, but I don't want to rush ahead. Fergus was kneeling on the damp grass under the windows of the east wing of the clinic, not knowing whether to laugh or cry, and I, desperately and (forever) futilely began to yell for a breast.

Of Aza nothing remained but one useless right rubber thong, which she carelessly threw into a corner before putting on her sneakers. She changed into the dress she had been wearing when the contractions started, when it was time to go to the hospital.

Not ten hours had passed since then. Everything went so fast, so smoothly, such a promising start and, what with all the hurry, it was lucky that the flat wasn't far from the hospital. Aza had stopped at the sink, legs apart, leaning forward and moaning in pain while a nervous Paul hurried to the hallway dresser looking for the envelope into which, in a moment of foresight weeks ago, he'd put aside the taxi money. But there was nothing in the drawer but rusty keys, broken pencils, a notepad full of scribbles, a greasy pack of cards and a few brittle rubber bands.

"Where's the damn envelope?" he shouted.

"Which arsehole stole my money," he bellowed.

Max and Irene looked out of their rooms and shrugged while Aza leaned sweating against the kitchen table. She was clasping her belly, as if it might fall off any moment.

"Calm down, Paul," Max said, and disappeared into the room to come out a couple of seconds later with a fistful of marks. Paul grabbed the money and the overnight bag that had been waiting for days now, just in case, next to the hallway dresser. He led Aza out of the apartment, slamming the door so hard behind them that a piece of wood fell off, next to the lock. It remained chipped until our commune split up and I, over my next six years, kept persistently scraping at it. It was the only visible scar that Aza had left.

"Is it time already?" Irene asked, yawning at Max.

"So crazy, right?"

In all the excitement over the impending birth, it hadn't occurred to Paul to unpack the overnight bag, which was still standing with locked zippers on one of the visitors' chairs in the hospital room. Hence, nobody realised

Stefanie Kremser

that Aza was swiftly and stealthily equipped with passport, a return ticket, wallet, toothbrush, toothpaste, skin cream, hairbrush, shampoo, two sets of underwear, a sweater and jogging pants, to disappear from our lives forever, without a word or as much as a backward glance.

Paul didn't suspect anything. He'd sneaked out of the hospital room when I was asleep and Aza was pretending to be because he urgently needed to be out in the fresh air, away from the stench of disinfectant, away from squeaky nurse steps on polished linoleum floors, away from the mouldy smell of bunches of flowers which visitors plonked down on every available surface. He walked the two blocks down to the café Ruffini, asked for a coffee, bought a packet of cigarettes from the vending machine and sat down by the window. It had stopped raining. Occasional drops splashed from gutters, beaded on bicycle saddles, and dribbled down windowpanes. Aza hadn't wanted him to be present at the birth and he, as if this was some bad seventies comedy, had waited in the passage, pacing up and down, smoking out the window and chewing gum. It had seemed like an eternity before Aza was at last trundled out of the delivery room, semi-conscious and with strands of sweaty hair stuck to her forehead. The midwife came too, holding me in her arms, and Paul took me without the slightest hesitation. He held me close and safe, as if he had spent his whole life doing only this. He gazed at me and beamed.

"My daughter," he whispered.

"My little one," he said, looking ecstatically at the midwife.

"My goodness. How tiny she is."

Then he cried a little bit, out of emotion, not knowing that he was going to shed many more tears that day. Right then, he only knew that everything was going to change, that everything was already different because a new life had irrevocably begun with me in the world.

My father sat in the Ruffini, wondering over his cup of coffee whether he could afford to invite the fifteen other café clients to a glass of Prosecco but then he remembered that he'd have to shout a round for Max and Irene too. And for his mates from volleyball. And for the man from the grocery store. Suddenly he needed to recall what I looked like. What was the colour of my eyes? Was my mouth heart-shaped like his, or straight, like Aza's? It startled him because he couldn't remember and this immediately drove him back to the hospital, with a completely new urge, even stronger than the crazy desire which had possessed him during the first weeks with Aza.

This was something else. This was love.

Looking up from the Orffstrasse, Paul could see from afar the upper floors of the hospital where he sought the window at the end of the hallway on the fifth floor. There was a burning sensation in his chest, which, for the first time, didn't feel oppressive but inspiring. Life with Aza hadn't been easy in the past few months but now, he thought, everything would be fine and maybe they'd even want to get married one day, although Paul wasn't so sure about that. Anyway, he wouldn't tell Max. That he'd ever wasted a thought on marriage would constitute a betrayal of their shared principles discussed at least once a week and late into the night at the kitchen table over a pot of chili con carne (marriage as a bourgeois institution, an instrument of oppression, restriction of freedom, a symbol of moral subjugation, et cetera, et cetera). Yet my father was basically a romantic, and exchanging rings or even a solemn signature was just as much part of that as his dream of a Tropical Institute, which he and Aza would run one day, carrying out research in the Amazon while my future siblings and I would play with children from some nearby naked Indian tribe, bristling with health under banana trees.

When Paul was about to cross a green square to reach the hospital he saw the police car at the entrance. The blue light revolved silently and there was a strange atmosphere, a mixture of seriousness and awe, a feeling that I'd have many years later when my mother had to decide whether I—for her—had survived or not. I'll come to this later. One thing at a time.

A dark-haired man with an oversized nose and jutting chin stood next to the police car, gesticulating as he spoke with one of the policemen. I was still screaming. Paul started to run. The inspirational fire in his chest held for a few more seconds, almost blasting him across the street before regressing back into the old anxiety, which, like a hard landing, threatened to pin him down on the sidewalk. A nurse held me in her arms as a doctor examined my neck, back, pelvis, legs. The woman from reception huddled in shared mute shock with the kiosk owner, the cleaning lady and another policeman. Only when the doctor gave a confident she's-okay nod did a murmur ripple through the group.

"*Chwała Bogu*," muttered the Polish cleaning lady.

"*Allaha Şükür*," said the Turkish kiosk owner.

"Thank God!" cried Nurse Marianne, plugging a bottle of milk into my mouth so I could finally relax and, slurping and sucking, unconcernedly enjoy my first dinner.

"What happened?" Paul asked.

"What about the baby?" he whispered.

Stefanie Kremser

"And Aza?"

The people gathered around me looked at my father in dismay. Finally it was Fergus who hugged him like a brother and reassured him.

"It's all right, mate," he soothed, after which he announced that, first of all, they could use a good beer. With a gesture the kiosk owner invited them into the hospital building.

"And then we'll talk about everything."

Lo-lee-lu, only the man in the moon is watching. I was given the name Luisa, called Lulu, and only the man in the moon knew where Aza was. This was my lullaby, and I was convinced that my father had made it up just for me. Lo-lee-lu: long lives Luisa.

I stayed two over-cautious weeks in the clinic so they could check for the slightest sign of concussion and help me to acquire the adaptability of a motherless only child, as well as a voracious appetite for milk substitutes. The midwife taught Paul how to feed me, to change nappies, bathe me, and the nurses were good to me. They rocked me in their arms, tickled my tummy and nuzzled my belly rolls so they'd remember my baby scent. I was visited by our flatmates Max and Irene, who bent over me with respectful distance and argued about who I'd look like. Paul already knew, but he kept it to himself. Later I'd spend hours in front of the mirror trying to imagine what my mother looked like, taking all the bits I didn't get from my father and fitting them together. Freckles and red hair for example. Dark skin. Otherwise . . . Well, I'd have to wait. There were no photos. There would be no memory, no stories.

"From here she looks like Aza," Max said and immediately regretted having mentioned her name.

"But if you look a bit from the right, she looks totally like you."

Irene said, "Hey Paul, so crazy, right?"

Then they were silent for a while.

"Who'll look after her now?"

When my grandparents came, Grandma immediately offered to take me to Mathildesberg, a village seven hundred kilometres from Munich. It was so close to Belgium that Grandpa could get their Sunday night chips just over the border before he bought the sausage on the way back in Mathildesberg's Currywurst booth. I went for the ride every time we visited them, hoping we'd meet some British soldiers in their grey-green trucks on the way and that they'd answer my friendly waving. Possibly—as a collective—they were my second love. My first love was Fergus, and at some point he taught me a few words so that, leaning out of the back window of Grandpa's car, I was able to address them in English.

"*Hallo*," I yelled into the wind, towards the military trucks. "How do you do!"

Paul had wanted to hear nothing of Grandma's and Grandpa's theories that it would be better for me to grow up in a small village like Mathildesberg rather than in a, well, turbulent city like Munich. He decided to finish university in Munich and, most importantly, to stay with me in the commune, no matter how difficult life might be for a penniless, single-parent biology student living with a bunch of constantly changing flatmates. He never explained why, although this was a question that could and had to be asked, because with me in Mathildeberg things would certainly have been easier. Grandma would have continued ironing at home for her neighbours while I would have been sitting at her feet watching the steam billowing from her ironing machine, which puffed and hissed and spat tiny drops that fell like dew on my outstretched palms. Grandpa would have continued as a postal worker in his one-man branch and come home for lunch. He would have given me a new stamp with a butterfly on it every day. In exchange, I'd have run down to the kiosk with two coins to buy him a cigar (plus one or two sticks of liquorice for me and some herbal sweets for Grandma). I would have been no trouble, occasioned no expense, and I would have added new meaning to their lives, a new goal, which they, now in their mid-forties, might well have needed. My father could have finished his studies in Aachen and come to us at weekends to help me practise cycling and walking on stilts every Saturday afternoon. But Paul had made his decision and only on my seventh birthday did I understand why. Until then, I yearned for each visit to Mathildesberg, bursting into tears at the farewells from Grandma and Grandpa who spoiled me rotten, much more than Max and Irene and all the others who came and went ever would have done.

Not that I was unhappy in the Munich flat, quite the opposite. I was Luisa, Lulu, Lu, a silent, smiling baby, and after long discussions with my grandparents and a quick democratic vote by our flatmates I was brought home to live with Paul, Max and Irene, two weeks after my birth, in a bright red stroller chosen by Grandma and paid for by Grandpa.

We lived in a spacious flat in the Nibelungenstrasse. The ochre-coloured, four-storey houses had been built in the nineteen thirties and, in summer, wild ivy crept across the windows. Roses bloomed in the front yard where children were not allowed to play. Instead we were allowed to do whatever we wanted in the backyard, which was pockmarked with gravel and mangy blotches of grass. The doors of our building were made of solid heavy wood and the wide stairs creaked when our neighbours climbed up to their respective flats. Max taught me later to identify every individual's steps, for example, those of Mrs. Blum from the third floor, whose court shoes barely touched the steps, so different from those of Mr. Schwarz, who slowly and heavily dragged himself up to the second floor. The easiest ones to recognise were the piano students who always dashed up to the flat directly above ours. They were late every day and tried to gain a few more seconds in the stairwell, loudly clattering up to the first floor. Shortly afterwards, when they'd shed their jackets and opened their music books, their playing began to sound over our heads.

The five of us lived on the ground floor sharing a ninety-square-metre, four-bedroom apartment. Sometimes there were six of us if a guest stayed on, which could mean for months because we were very tolerant. The guests usually slept in the box room, which really didn't really count as a room as it had just enough space for a narrow bunk and a bedside table. It could also happen that the guest had invited another guest who then also remained, without any vote being taken on the matter, for days or even weeks. That was fine as long as they helped with the rent, which was still fairly affordable. With me, my father, Fergus, Irene, Max, the guest and the guest's friend, there were sometimes up to seven of us sitting in the kitchen for a late Saturday breakfast, pooling whatever everyone had brought, things like honey, fresh bread or stuffed grape leaves from the market, so that all sorts of ill-matched, sweet and savoury goodies were placed on the table. Each of us had his or her own taste: a bit Bavarian with white sausage and sweet mustard, a bit English with scrambled eggs and bacon, a bit homey with someone's mother's jam, a bit of solidarity with the supposedly multicultural society, which was no more than a vague idea in the form of feta cheese, Turkish bread, hummus and mozzarella and, occasionally, some kind of exotic fruit that no one quite knew how to peel. I remember well our richly endowed kitchen table, cigarette butts pressed into empty eggshells, the mixed smells of coffee and wheat beer, the array of chipped mugs and always blunt knives that were pushed out of reach whenever I made a grab at them. I remember sitting on Paul's lap as he fed me applesauce while Irene let him have a puff of one of the cigarettes she rolled, which she gently pushed between his lips. After a while, Paul passed me on and so I did the rounds, sitting on warm laps letting everyone play with me as if I were a doll: arms up and down, feet up and down, I was tickled and sniffed, or lifted into the air by Fergus, until they'd had enough of me and got bored. Then they deposited me in the playpen, which was either in Paul's room or in the hallway. No matter how unthinkable it was for them having or wanting to take care of a child, there was always someone to keep an eye on me.

Max was most often at home. He had founded the commune three years earlier when he moved from Rosenheim to Munich, where he studied at the Art Academy. Skinny and chain-smoking, he sat for hours and hours at his drawing table. He was a comic book artist, a genius in typography, a chronicler of stories that bloomed from his small-town loneliness. With only a ruler, a pencil and an ink pen, he managed to perfect an art, which, in Germany, was yet to have a name: the graphic novel. When Max was working in his room, I crawled on to his futon and pressed my head into the pillow, thinking I was hiding. When I was older, I lay on the floor and, tongue stuck out, scribbled on the back of the sheets of paper that he gave me. Later, when I'd learned how to submit hand to will, he gave me discarded drawings from a stash he kept in a drawer for me to colour in. We spent many days together like this, sharing his pencils and our silence, which was broken now and then by the rustling of the bag of prunes, the sound of his lighter clicking into flame and Max's occasional inquiries as to whether everything was all right.

"Hungry, Lulu?"

"Thirsty?"

"Sleep?"

"Another prune?"

Thanks to all the prunes Max gave me in form of juice, mousse and later in whole, pitted form, I had perfectly functioning bowels and never complained of stomachache. I know how difficult it would have been to take me on as a long-term project if I'd suffered from wind or earache, if I'd been a crying baby or a grizzling toddler. But I was lucky—we were all very lucky—so, since I was always calm and happy and liked to play alone for hours, no one thought about the fact that it might have been different. Which means that I was really part of their lives. I was one of them.

Where do I start? With whom? With Aza, who walked away? With Fergus, who came? With Irene, who didn't make it, or with Max, who did? With my father and me, who stayed until the end?

I'll take things one at a time and promise to do my best. Autumn begins in a sunny mood, and I'm three weeks old. If you stay too long under the linden trees you get sticky hair. Swans are paddling up and down

Stefanie Kremser

Nymphenburg canal, and Aza is in the middle of nowhere. We are in our Munich apartment with the worn wooden floors and have an empty room, which was Aza's for eight months but is now being paid by Paul. We have several problems. I'll start with the least of them: we are looking for a new tenant.

The solution came one wonderful morning. I was draped across my father's chest in my sling, listening to the Breakfast Symphony of kitchen noises being performed all around me in the gurgling of sink water, water boiling in the kettle, clatter of plates and cups, Cat Stevens' *Peace Train* chugging away, riding on the edge of darkness in the radio to the accompaniment of Irene's husky, melodious *laaa-la-lala-laa* (ride on the peace train) *pa pa pa pa*. Max washed the breakfast dishes while Paul took the whistling kettle off the burner to sterilise my bottles. Dangling there against his belly, blinking myopically up at his eyes, I balled my fists around a sunbeam that dropped through the strands of his dark hair.

Irene, as usual, did nothing. She lolled on the sofa we had installed in our kitchen, rolled cigarettes and was the first to come up with a proposal.

"His name is Francesco. He works in the Venezia ice cream parlour and needs a place till December."

"Forget it," said Max. "You just want to get into bed with him."

"Anyway, what are we supposed to do after December?" Paul asked.

"But he looks so incredibly good," pleaded Irene.

They glanced at each other, wordlessly voted two against one, and the ice cream man was no longer an issue for either Paul or Max.

"And what about Luisa?" Irene protested. "She has a right to vote too, and kids love ice cream. And Italians love kids!"

"Lulu is three weeks old," Paul pointed out. "She's a baby. Babies don't eat ice cream."

Irene didn't have a chance, not even with me as another woman, so to speak, who could have shown some solidarity. Could have. If I'd wanted to, but I didn't because I didn't want a stranger, didn't want Francesco, or Claudia, who Max now suggested, once Francesco had been discarded. She was also someone who apparently looked insanely good, was a fellow student at the Art Academy and Max naturally wanted to get into bed with her, and so on and so forth. It wasn't easy for my father, who'd gone through the painful experience of being roughly thrust into maturity on the day of my birth, and who now suffered from needing to be responsible. But for me, with the same burning desire for responsibility plus honest devotion, it wasn't easy either. No, I didn't want new faces. I didn't want more flatmates who'd be more or less disinterested in me. I wanted my tea leaf–scented Englishman, who, by then, had visited me three times, bringing touchingly meaningless gifts. A sunflower for Paul, which wilted in an empty milk bottle for two weeks. A foam rubber rugby ball, which Max accidentally threw out of the kitchen window to languish forevermore where it landed. Or the tin of Scottish shortbread that Irene ravenously devoured when she was high. And now someone rang the doorbell, just when we were voting for or against Claudia and, just as I'd been hoping, Fergus appeared, bringing me a stretched wine gum decorated with specks of tobacco, which he pulled out of his jacket pocket with every intention of sticking it in my mouth. In his other hand he held a bulging backpack with a pair of old sneakers strapped to it.

"Man!" said my father, "Don't tell me you're going back to England?"

Fergus put the bag down and shook his head.

"It's over. She kicked me out. It's not even been a month, man. Hello Lu, my baby. Oh, of course, she can't eat that, right?"

He bit the wine gum, sucking on it and pulling the bottom half down his chin. As he closed the door behind him, he left the gum hanging out of his mouth. He looked so helpless, a lovesick giant who'd lost his appetite but who, aware of his preordained duty in the fairy tale, had half swallowed a dwarf, which was still jiggling its little legs.

"I'm really sorry," said my father, and he meant it. He knew what abandonment felt like. This was an issue as serious and painful as the question of the meaning of life, about which he was not willing to talk, not yet. But he understood, and Fergus nodded gratefully. We all pondered the matter for a while. Paul straightened me in the sling; Max wiped his hands on the tea towel he'd thrown over his shoulder; Irene moistened her cigarette paper with the tip of the tongue. Fergus kept sucking on the half-eaten wine-gum dwarf.

"Yes," he finally summed up, because silence, too, has a beginning, a middle and an end.

"Yes," said Paul.

"Wow," Irene chimed in.

Fergus sighed. "You wouldn't have a place for me to kip down?" he asked at precisely the same time as Paul asked, "Why don't you stay a while with us?"

They laughed. It was nice that Paul had the same idea. Maybe it was just a hunch, but at least it also showed presence of mind and it was a happy chance for him to express his gratitude to Fergus at last. There was no

Stefanie Kremser

question about helping him. It was a fact. I mean, it was like when I was at Grandma and Grandpa's, and I didn't have to ask for a woodruff-flavoured popsicle but was simply allowed to take one out of the freezer in the basement (if I dared to go down there alone). The fact that they had bright green woodruff-flavoured ice cream in the freezer even before I knew this was my favourite flavour was proof that some answers exist before their questions. It was the same thing with Fergus and my father.

After Paul and Fergus met on the day of my birth, there was an unspoken closeness between them, yes, almost intimacy, nourished by Fergus' instinct to help more than was actually humanly possible and by Paul's impulse to consider him, from the first pat on the shoulder, as a natural part of his, of our lives. Fergus had been there in the right place at the right time, as they say, and we couldn't help but hold him in our hearts, in Paul's which, so empty, so hollow, was suddenly beating, and in mine, which, although no bigger than a butterfly, had space for a whole world.

Apart from the Turkish kiosk owner who constantly forced chocolate on them, hoping to dispel the bitterness of what happened, and who constantly threw his hands heavenwards, thanking God for his help, Fergus was the only person who'd witnessed Paul at the point of disintegration. My father, shaken by all the possible consequences, kept imagining me plummeting down five floors. What if Fergus hadn't been there . . . and how could Aza . . . why, just why? On that fresh, rain-scented summer evening Paul sat shattered and in tears on a soft-drinks crate under the flickering neon of the hospital kiosk, riding waves of horror and gratitude and shame. Horror at the thought that Fergus might not have been in the right place at the right time; gratitude that he had been there; and shame, yes, even that was related with Fergus, because Paul believed he would never again have the strength to lift such a heavy thing as a bottle of beer, let alone get it up to his mouth. But there are moments that weld things together, and this was such a moment. Fergus lent my father not only his ear, listening patiently, nodding and giving him an encouraging pat on the shoulder every now and then, but he also handed him a bottle, at exactly the same moment as I got mine from Nurse Marianne in the neonatal unit.

Fergus moved into Aza's room. He didn't need much: a mattress, some borrowed towels, bed linen, a clothes rack and a table lamp, which he placed on an upturned orange crate next to the bed. Irene gave him one of her potted cannabis plants, whose spicy fragrance helped me fall asleep when Fergus took me in on the odd occasion when Paul had a nocturnal visitor. Later, in a superannuated armchair that Fergus retrieved from the rubbish dump a few blocks away, I pulled myself up to stand unsteadily on my own for the first time. The purple flowery fabric of the armchair was threadbare at the edges and I loved poking my fingers inside the bursting seams, interring marbles inside it or hoarding coins that had rolled out of Fergus' pocket behind the seat cushion and which he, with his broad hands as big as I was once small, couldn't fish out.

So he came and went, came and went, came and stayed. Fergus and his ex reconciled four more times, but he didn't give up the room until he had to return to South East London one day. But that's still a long way off and, for the time being, we need to know that he stayed almost seven years, and I learned that love, like the meaning of life, is as serious and painful an issue as abandonment, and that you can love even if you've been abandoned, and that you can leave even if you love.

——

Stefanie Kremser

then touch me here

(ten poems)

EDVĪNS RAUPS

Edvīns Raups was born in Sigulda in 1962 and studied English language and literature at the University of Latvia. He is one of the great innovators in Latvian poetry, giving back to the language its metaphysical purity and delight. As Latvian literary critic Guntis Berelis observes, "Raups liberates words from the world, and his poetry is made up of visions and perceptions. ('Only by closing your eyes can you see'). As soon as a word loses its connection with the world of objects, it retreats into itself; paradoxically, this retreat saturates a word with an infinite number of new meanings, and the word can be perpetually born anew."

Translated from Latvian by Margita Gailitis.

I KNOW EVERYTHING
ABOUT NOTHING THAT'S HOW IT IS
A GULL SWIMS
ON THE ARMS OF A WAVE
KILI KILI

This era
you measure in sinews
which tense
when waking conquers the night
    You walk behind the falling autumn leaves
with a torch raised high
and play the madwoman
for whom nothing on this earth seems strange
    in the morning
everything again will be fine
my dear death
    You whose elbows in sleep
lie helpless
by your side allow me
to deny
the dream
    What use your high forehead
when belief's empty caravan chases
its horses downward
into a Triad

    and the only thing human in you
is quick anger
    You! slave driver Eritrea
I fall at your feet like
cool dew on a linden's
forked branch
    Craving water
great bodies of water love
and ships

We two alone are
colored antinational baroque
saving our will
       for something supernaturally simple
we dissolve in emotion

    I
a bystander
gladly sneak into our presence Without
    a sound to flow away into existence
        together with our ancestors
after a battle with the sun.

      We two
whose souls can't keep together
discarded like the Pope's Bulls While
      cicadas susurrate about lyrical milk
      fed pigs in distant Jerusalem
and crowds of daisies

          right here
in Archbishop Meinhard's rational cell
opposite the Daugava Boulevard

     I
don't want to take a break
having fallen for your levy
    like a blossoming cluster of heaven
     like a Slav stork
atop a heartpole

      Let it happen
to my remains
let every grain of sand be like a pain
    plaster I am an empire
        you—the ruin
we're made for each other

Note: During the Crusades of the twelfth century, in 1186, the Pope appointed Meinhard as the first bishop to Latvia (then Livonia) to Christianize the Baltic tribes. He was eventually made archbishop and canonized.

Edvīns Raups

my colors the combination
of field plants and hills like veins And
the veining collects into scars
round the centre of the lake in the morning
when chatter chatter come the shakes
shivering oh Blood mother
whispers stay in your place stand
like a pillar put in a word for the child
for me And suddenly all changes gender
and number and God's frogs
leap about *kerplunk* yes water
it's good she says but don't While the owl
still is blind While there are drying sheds
for hay and each of us is through
our own straw dying
upwards

a reflection erodes the edge of the lake
reaches further stretches out hands
beyond the circle at this moment
either a cool wing or a shadow
lying across the breast which calmly
and harmoniously responds
to a pulse balances light
streams and slowly floods
into matter scattering ashes
which make my beloved at the lake
shore large
in my heart . . .

Edvīns Raups

a tiny tiny girl
bends her fingers
as if in a film counts
time She
makes a full stop with her curtsey
a whisper rustles
there's just an inkling
someone should
find me

       See
an overabundance of shattered hope
settle into the empty cheeks of the apple tree
and She blossoms
shows me
a singular possibility and such brilliance!
birds roost on the bridge line
formed by our noses
sand
I remember well greater floods once
and many misfortunes that remained
hidden
for life
yes a mollusk gazes from his shell
a martin catches moments in the air
her fledglings fed
see what an overabundance of shattered hope
settles deep in the sharp rocky shore at river bends
and everything flows
away smoothly

Only a dark bruise at the temples!
mundane longing
for the absolute gifts me with a horizon scar
which you tie round
your waist and something
moves
within you
phooey! It's a branch
in the apple tree's crown
in search
       of a moving experience

heart-clear
coals
burning in an emptiness Birds
with crooked beaks
advertised
a just court
and you danced
as if for the first time tempted
by the future—

My Lord
My angel! You stay
in your place.

I won't stay

A heron
a heron tilts back
his head his Larynx
bulges like a bone
of sadness On
the horizon
line And
the mind clenches
into a fist
uktah
lulu

the wholeness
of heaven overflows
in you and
you get up As if
called
in the dark While
she hurries
beauty Out
to where Hands curve
into a circle And
e m b r a c e which Reason
can not.

———

The Heart of Man

(novel excerpt)

JÓN KALMAN STEFÁNSSON

Jón Kalman Stefánsson was born in Reykjavik in 1973. His novels, as *La Repubblica* describes them, are derived from an "extreme viewpoint where man is left to his own devices, facing a world much greater than himself; a world that for him has neither cure, nor love, but offers him only the changing seasons. *Hjarta Mansinns (The Heart of Man)* . . . centres around the ancient notion of the solitude of man, in an Iceland made of fishermen and wind, and the tenuous attachment to life. Because of this, man seeks friendship or love, even though he realises that this is futile."

Translated from Icelandic by Philip Roughton.

WORDS ARE NOT LIFELESS ROCK or gnawed and wind-whitened bones up in the mountains. Even the most mundane of them can grow distant over time and transform into museums that house the past, what is gone and will never return. Meadows, manured hayfields, we're moved to tears by these words, something snaps within us, as when we unexpectedly come across old photos and see faces long since lost in the earth, or the sea. Where are the meadows?, and we recall tranquil summer mornings, so still and deep that we could nearly hear God, but we also recall the toil, the wet feet, the wet grass, newly mown, how tremendously we recall the fatigue, we recall what's gone and will never return, recall so poignantly that we were once alive, that we could once hold hands, that there were once childish questions. Once we were alive, once had names and they were sometimes spoken in such a way that the deserts of life began to flourish with green. Once we were alive, but not any longer, what surrounds us is called death. Where are the meadows?

· · · · ·

IS YOUR HEART STILL BEATING?

And how does it beat?

Damn it all. The boy receives a letter in which he's asked about his heartbeat. As if living isn't enough of a trial.

He wakes up each morning just before six, reaches out and grabs a book, poems to read as he emerges from his dreams into the delicate morning, connecting night and day, dreams and waking with poems, there may be no better way for a person to wake up. Yet the questions don't go anywhere, what is he supposed to do with his life?, does he love Ragnheiður, whom he's met twice since returning from his journey with Jens, a journey that went all the way to the end of the world, through gloomy weather, through life and death. The first time, they met on the street and she looked at the boy as if he were nothing, and even a little less than that. The next day he was about to enter the German Bakery when Ragnheiður stepped out with Danish pastries for her father, Friðrik, warm pastries were practically the only luxury he permitted himself and Ragnheiður the only one who was allowed to buy them, and then she wanted to get to know the boy, I heard you nearly killed yourself on your journey with the drunkard, how could you ever think of dying before I left for Copenhagen? Jens is not a drunk, he said, feeling mildly dizzy, her eyes are somewhat wide-set, those grey eyes that can be cold as frost, as the blood of a cod; between them dwells my fate, he thought, nothing I can do about it. This is a new sweater, she said, yes, he said. It's beautiful, they know how to clothe you, you've got dandruff on your shoulder, said Ragnheiður, brushing off his right shoulder.

Is your heart still beating? And why?

Life is strange; as far back as he can remember, education had been the promised land that echoed under and over his mother's letters—his only education until now had been in preparation for his confirmation, and one month of lessons with an itinerant teacher when he was ten or twelve years old. Yet he was able to read and write fluently by the time the sea claimed his father, and he practiced writing whenever he could, scratched letters on ice, on mouldering rafters in the roof of the cowshed, in the snow, at first without constraint, neglected his chores, the rafters barely held up against the weight of the words, and one morning when people came out of the farmhouse it was nearly impossible for them to step into the snow due to the sheer amount of words, the boy hadn't been able to sleep because of the moonlight, had gone out while it was still night and started to write. Twelve strokes of the switch for three days in a row and no dinner brought him to his senses. He was beaten, not out of malice but necessity, for, in the first place, writing words in the snow or dirt is bad luck, and second, his chores went unattended in the meantime, and how were people supposed to live in this land if they neglected their work? And what would happen to you, who would employ you if word got round that you wrote in the snow instead of worked, you'd soon end up on the parish, you'd be kicked at like a dog, so welcome these twelve strokes, let them teach you, they're not given out of malice, but necessity, even care. But now he wakes up, does light chores, takes lessons twice a week from Gísli, the most educated man in the Village, the county, even this quarter of the country, the headmaster himself, has English lessons twice a week with Hulda, occasionally arithmetic with Helga, wakes up in the mornings, connects dreams and reality with poems, reality where he's encouraged to get an education, what is distant has come to him, yet he asks, why am I alive, where is life heading? And then the boy receives a letter.

Is your heart still beating?

And if so, how?

It's beating like that of a drowning man, a wingless bird, how the hell should he answer this? But of course it's important to receive a letter, to have a person consider it worthwhile enough to be willing to sit down and draw up words and have you in mind the entire time it takes to write the letter, to receive a letter indicates that you exist, that you're closer to being light than darkness. Admittedly, not all letters are good, and some should perhaps never have been sent, never have been opened, read, some are full of hatred, accusations, they're poison that will deprive you of all your strength, they bring darkness and disappointment.

There's a letter for you, said Andrea, with something of a sarcastic look. Letter?, he exclaimed in surprise, because who should be writing him a letter, his mother sent him eleven letters, he has all of them, the twelfth never came. It might be from Reverend Kjartan, he said nonchalantly, and absurdly, of course; why should Reverend Kjartan send him a letter, why should such an educated, intelligent man, the owner of large numbers of books, show such an interest in his existence? Might be from Reverend Kjartan, he said, having just come into the café after an English lesson with Hulda, two English lessons behind him, singular, plural, the definite and indefinite articles, a table, tables, an apple, apples. Have you tasted an apple?, asked the boy as he wrote down the word for this spherical, exotic fruit, as far from our everyday existence as Jupiter. No, said Hulda curtly, telling a lie. Teitur sometimes gets apples from foreign sailors who've come here often and might be called acquaintances of his, but it's easier to say no; it's safer, no is a fort protecting her. No, she says, and you can't get any closer. No, said Hulda, glancing at the boy through the battlements, and he said, unable to refrain from doing so, is there a plural form of love in every language? A love, she said, loves. With a "v"? Yes, "v," but you shouldn't write it down, it's not in the curriculum. Love isn't in the curriculum? No, just apples, she replied, glancing down to hide her smile.

Reverend Kjartan?, asked Andrea. He's in Vík, remember, Jens and I stayed there our second night, his wife's name is Anna, and she's nearly blind. Yes, no, the letter's hardly from him, it's from a woman, or at least a woman has addressed the envelope. A woman?, he said in surprise, umm, oh, then that would be María, from Vetrarströnd. He took the envelope, gave it a quick look and was taken aback when he saw the letters, their ardour, as if they were all running into each other. They're fighting, he added; the letters, he explained, when Andrea asked, What? So she's that ardent, is she?, said Andrea, smiling at the boy, who heard hardly anything over the pounding of his heart. María would never write like that; she's ardent, of course, fires burn inside her, she cries sometimes about something she's lacking, without knowing what, just feels as if she's lacking something, and then Jón holds her, his embrace is warm and strong, yet doesn't encompass the horizon. No, María would likely be more meticulous, she delivers only the best and would have made the letters smaller, to save space; she knows no other way. He looked at the envelope. Yes, he said, she's ardent. How does her heart beat? So ardently that herbivores in Africa look up, so ardently that the birds of the air are knocked off course. We can go over English a bit, said the boy to Andrea, who smiled widely, warming the boy with her smile, warming him so much that he was able to sit at the table, go over singular and plural in English without going mad with impatience, he sat calmly, now and then leaning closer to Andrea, she has such a warm scent, blended with a faint musty smell from her basement room, and twice she stroked his cheek with her weary fingers, these two people far out on life's sea of uncertainty, surrounded by heavy currents. He breathed in Andrea and the letter quivered as it touched his flesh.

But now he's sitting in his room. Is your heart beating?

· · · · ·

"IS YOUR HEART STILL BEATING? And if so, how? I'm sitting against the wall of the house, the same one you crashed into, you and the big man, Jens. It's sunny and everything is very wet. Your feet get wet just by looking out. But now the sun is warm. You can give it that. The frost melts into the ground. That's why the ground is wet, as if it's crying. I'm sitting on a stool. I brought a book with me to read, I wasn't going to write you a letter, the book is a bit thick. It's called *The Odyssey* and is age-old. Steinunn said it was a "classic"; I expect that you know something about it. That's how you are. I noticed it immediately. That's why you know it's about a man who's trying to make it home, but who ends up in all sorts of adventures and catastrophes. In the meantime his wife has to wait at home, albeit in a palace and with enough to eat, it's warm there and no one gets buried in snow. Yet it's probably no easier to exist there, it's probably no easier to wait in uncertainty though the weather is good and the house doesn't leak. I would never believe it were easier. She has to wait and doesn't even know whether he's dead or is being unfaithful to her with other women. She just waits, composed and patient and faithful, while he undergoes adventures, and then a book is written about him. No need to tell me about women. No need to tell me about men. Then it crossed my mind to write you a letter. I guess I'd thought about you, I must have, but that doesn't have to mean anything. For example, I also think about the frost that melts into the ground and makes everything wet, makes all our feet wet. Yet not yours, you who had such good shoes, people here still talk about it, and then there are those American boots that apparently keep one's feet eternally dry. Not many people here believe it. But even if I think about you, it's absolutely meaningless. So much has been thought here in Iceland, ever since the country was settled a thousand years ago. Yet some people never seem to think anything, simply never. Have you noticed that? The expressions of such people remind me of rotten, useless hay. I'm going to stop now. Sometimes I also think about horse trailers, about kittens and about Jupiter, which is a very big planet yet is still just a tiny speck of light in the sky. I also think sometimes about the rain in China, I'm sure you're familiar with it. I think about all sorts of things. So even if I think about you, it's nothing remarkable. I'm sitting on a stool, no, I'd already mentioned that. The snow is melting on the mountain above me. You see how little happens here. Life here is just melting snow and frost. Is it any wonder that it crossed my mind to write a letter? I'm lying, though. Life here isn't just melting snow and frost. For example, the shop manager Sigurður is drunker some days than others. Yesterday he couldn't stand on his own two feet. The day before yesterday he was so spirited that his wife had to lock him in the house. She seems to have some trick or other for keeping him inside when it's really necessary. That Hjalti who was with you still hasn't been found. The doctor and his wife sent some men over to Nes. What a place that's supposed to be. The men said that when they got there, they found no Hjalti, but that everyone was doing well. People can be so stupid. They might have been standing upright, but of course they weren't doing well. Maybe I should go there and never come back? I wonder if you've recovered? You two didn't look entirely well when you left. There was still a chill in you, and particularly in the big man, Jens. He made it all the way home. His sister was so terribly happy. She's considerably better than us, from the sound of it. You see that I've come to the end of this sheet of paper, there's no more space. Nor can I spend more time on it. I know that I can't write, you don't need to tell me. My letters are as ugly and tattered as old hens."

$$\cdots\cdots$$

I THINK ABOUT YOU SOMETIMES. It's good to walk up over the Village where the tussocks are soft, you lie down between them and it's as if they embrace you. The boy is lying between them, looking at the sky. I think about you sometimes. Then it occurred to me to write you a letter. Which means I'd thought about you. He lies there so long that the birds have started to become used to him; even the redshank has calmed down. But I also think sometimes about a horse trailer, about kittens and about Jupiter, which is a very big planet yet is still just a tiny speck of light in the sky. I also think about rain in China, I'm sure you're familiar with it.

Helga bristles when he returns; what's the meaning of disappearing like that?, there are things needing doing here, the boy replies with an indecipherable mutter, so pale and muddleheaded that Helga says, well then, and sends him to the café. It's as if she knows how he feels, as if she understands his sensitivity. Sensitivity is my truest dream, says an old poem, a line that shines through time, and it's true, the essence of man is sensitivity, we feel it so desperately in the spring when existence is at the needlepoint of life and death. The song of the plover, that poignant sound, reminds us of it and now and then we're startled to hear it, it's why Ólafur sat down up on the mountainside, in sleet, and wept; he had to weep, he sensed man's truest dream while realizing how much distance there is between his dream and the world that he's created. And then it's evening.

It's evening, and the weather is bad, those who are able to be at home are at home, listening to the wind, reading *The Will of the People*; Icelanders, it says, appear to have stepped up and sworn a solemn vow to live beyond their means, under the control of merchants, and then die in debt. Merchants rule our days, because we allow them to. People believe that it's an unconquerable law. Consequently, we don't stand together; everyone lives for himself. And therewith, we nearly always fish using their hooks, not our own. Skúli owns a share in a schooner, his father-in-law is a wealthy farmer in a bountiful area south of the mountains, Skúli can afford to provoke us with his pen, having little to lose, which is different than us, who depend entirely on merchants and their goodwill. It not like it isn't fun to read such things: it's titillating, exciting, a bit like when children go off somewhere to say bad words. It's good when someone gives others what for; it makes them tremble a bit.

Dogs have to have the chance to bark now and then, says Friðrik; then there's less chance they'll bite. It's evening, terribly windy, pelting rain, out of the question to open the windows, the cigar smoke hangs thickly in Friðrik's master bedroom, so big it's nearly a parlour. There are six of them:

Friðrik, Reverend Þorvaldur, Dr. Sigurður, Jón, the factor of Léo's Shop and Trading Company, the magistrate Lárus, and Högni, the head book-keeper in Tryggvi's Shop and Trading Company and director of the Savings Bank, which opened three years ago; it's open for business an hour a day, five days a week. Lárus had started talking about one of Skúli's articles; he's becoming more and more aggressive, said the magistrate, before list-ing various other articles, and Friðrik simply let them talk, allowed them to worry, he's grown dangerous, said Sigurður, who always sits so bloody straight, yes, says Jón, excitedly, sucking on his cigar, Skúli's what you call in Danish a *skadefugl*—a curmudgeon—and the others smile at the word, as if Tove were speaking through him, but then the door opens and a maid en-ters with more coffee, refills their cups, adds to their cognac glasses; she's young, moves lithely, like a herb in water, never looks up, they don't get to see her eyes properly, those blue stones, and she doesn't let it perturb her though they all look, watch her as the fire works its way up their stiff cigars, with a low hiss, but she's glad to get out of there. A fine piece of work, mut-ters Lárus; to say the least, agrees Sigurður, while Þorvaldur says nothing, having simply watched like the others, that was his praise, and then Friðrik says, at first waving his hand as if to brush the girl aside, her youth, the agitation that they all felt, dogs have to be allowed to bark, then there's less chance they'll bite. But Skúli hit the nail precisely on the head, albeit in reverse; most people spend more than they have, as witnessed clearly in the trading companies' ledgers, far too many die in debt, which is why we must keep a firm hand on things, otherwise all of society will resemble the ledgers of its people—full of nothing but debt. But never mind Skúli, he's no threat; it's Geirþrúður we need to worry about. Skúli hides nothing, is plain for all to see, but she's underhanded, shrewder, causes a stir, and is corruptive to good morals, no less. You remember how she got her hands on Kolbeinn's share when he lost his vision, acquired a substantial majority in one of the Village's best ships by inviting him to live with her? It doesn't cost much to feed blind wretches, wretches who also have plenty of their own money; where's it supposed to go when they breathe their last, huh? She's clever and takes advantage of situations. She got hold of Snorri's share in the ice-house for a bargain two years ago, tossed him a pittance of a payment, he was and is no man to make stipulations and was surely overjoyed to get at least something out of it, while she tightened the noose around the ruffian's neck, and is likely lying in wait now for his schooner, the *Hope*, if she hasn't already secured it; in her own opinion, adds Friðrik. Has Tryggvi got his eye on Snorri's company?, asks Jón; he has to ask, has

Jón Kalman Stefánsson

been ordered to ask. Friðrik looks at him, smokes, the rain beats down on the house, it's a June evening.

It's the very start of June, yet it's still dusky between the mountains. Gloomy weather. The wind picks up, the saltfish stacks are tied down tightly. There's hardly anyone out and about in this tempest, despite the day beginning beautifully, the sky full of sun and blue promises of calm and comfort, birdsong audible far and wide, nothing to hinder the transparent, motionless air. Flies buzzed over flowers and grass, saltfish covered the spit, the drying lots, much had turned green and beautiful in the mountains. In the Village itself, all was astir, naturally; there were shouts and cries and laughter and cursing and hands that moved. Lúlli and Oddur were on a tear down in the hold of a ship, its captain rode off with Geirþrúður; I could love this country, he said. They rode up onto a heath, down into another fjord and into an empty, grassy valley.

There's good cover here, said Geirþrúður, and he gave her a long look before saying that he could love this country. Everything was turning green, and it was still and quiet between the tussocks, between the blades of grass, between the mountains that gathered sunshine and shone. On such days it's as if the birdsong can heal the wounds within us. They lay in the grass for a long time, found a hollow, those who find good hollows during an Icelandic summer can't complain, bliss awaits them, that is, if the birds let them be. The blades of grass move almost imperceptibly, like rows of venerable statesmen, and the birdsong healed wounds. I could easily love this country, said the captain, before adding, I could easily love you. People say the most incredible things before achieving satisfaction for their desires, or during, all that's been whispered, breathless phrases, immensely deep promises that prove to be shallow and worth little when all is said and done, the orgasm done and gone, the penis no longer erect and quivering with ardour and the lust for life, but instead slack, a dangling rag of skin between the legs. But the moment had passed when he said he could love her. They'd lain down and nearly ripped off their clothing, which was in their way, it was unbridled passion, it was vehemence, the sky witnessed it, the blades of grass felt it, the mountains heard it and it startled nearby birds; they were like wild animals, they were beautiful, but now it was over. They smoked, sipped from a flask, gazed at blades of grass, the sky, the mountain, birds, and the captain said that he could love her.

He lay with his head in her lap and she stroked the hair back from his forehead, his eyes, those pure eyes, from that strong, beautiful face, stroked the lips that knew so well how to kiss, knew how to speak words that were good to hear. I know, she said. You could love me, he said, he asked, he begged. A woman in love is defenceless, she said, and I can't take that chance, and besides, you're married, you love your wife; continue to do so. Are you cruel, perhaps? No, but life can easily be so. And then he was sad, a bit like a child, this big foreigner, captain of a substantial sailing ship that Lúlli and Oddur worked on emptying while its captain lay with Geirþrúður among tussocks, beneath the blue sky. Did you get to put your arms around her?, repeated Lúlli, having to press his friend hard to get an answer, and finally Oddur answered; he smiled.

Can a man love two women?, asked the captain. I expect so, she said, her long fingers in his thick hair, and perhaps even more if there's an ocean between them. But you don't know me, John, I'm just a diversion in your life, a little adventure on a long sea-voyage, a little dusky adventure that awaits you here at the end of the world, in among such steep, high mountains that no one can see us. You couldn't love me, not if you knew me, were with me every day, my heart is an organ that beats because it can do no other. I'm a sea, John, and as the sea grants you freedom for a little while, I offer you adventure, a touch of sin, yet those who venture too far out onto such oceans, and for too long, find little but loneliness and death.

A snipe whinnied close by, a plover replied with a poignant cry. Are you so unhappy?, he asked softly, he asked tenderly. You need to experience happiness to understand unhappiness, and don't look at me like that, no one needs to comfort me, there's nothing to comfort, life is either victory or defeat, not happiness or unhappiness, and I'm going to be victorious in my own way. How can you be victorious without happiness?, asked her captain, John Andersen, lifting his thick hands and stroking Geirþrúður's eyes, stroking tenderly, stroking as a man strokes something that matters a great deal to him, and she took his hand, bit it lightly with her predator's teeth, I'll tell you tomorrow, or whisper it to you, but now it's getting colder. And they both looked up at the sky, the blueness had darkened, the storm pounding Friðrik's house was approaching. But if you want, she added, and if you can manage again, I'm ready. Only if I may love you, he said.

You may; but then leave your love behind when you sail away, leave it here between the mountains.

Love is not a thing that one lays aside.

Yes, this love is, she said, unbuttoning her blouse. She unbuttoned her blouse and he beheld her gleaming white breasts, those breasts that he could gaze at endlessly, that pursued him far out to sea, all the way to England, those breasts, that skin, that scent, those long legs that locked around him, and the pitch-black hair that flowed like darkness over green heather and grass, those hoarse words that she muttered in his ear, if I could only love you, he whispered happily, he whispered despairingly; it would be only unhappiness and death, she whispered back, before forcing his head down to prevent him from seeing her face, seeing the black eyes that looked up at the sky. The sky that was growing restless. The sky that is so distant it seems at times to have sentenced man to solitude.

And now this sky is heavy and restless, with dark, rushing clouds. It's summer, yet dangerous weather hangs over us. In June, which be so bright that it seems we can see to the bottom of existence, even as if we can see eternity, friendly and huge in the distance. A storm, yet in June; it could certainly treat us more fairly.

The wind breaks up the sea and all that is loose blows away: handcarts, shovels, promises; forgive me, but I don't love you anymore, the wind tore my love from me, blew it away. Horses stand on the moors, in some places completely exposed, turning away from the wind that lashes all of nature, they let the tempest pass over them, stare straight ahead, look forward to grazing again. The rain pounds on them violently, it pounds on the big parlour window in Geirþrúður's house, all four of them sit in the parlour, the boy beneath a dim lamp, you've got to have light to see the pages; whither went the light, who took it, bring it back, we don't deserve this.

He has to sharpen his voice somewhat for the three of them to hear, because all the words have to come across, that's how poetry is, those are the rules, that's how it should be, must be, writing is a war and maybe authors experience more defeat than victory, that's just how it is, Gísli had explained, losing himself in his explanation, there was a gleam in his eye, as if he were really alive. He'd read over the five pages that the boy had translated of Mr. Dickens' story, *A Tale of Two Cities*. It was the best of times, it was the worst of times. In this story there are few mistakes, few defeats, making the job of the translator more difficult, yet happier. The boy said nothing, had the five pages in front of him, in some places marked up by Gísli, the translation, the tireless work, anguish, sweat, joy, delicate movement between languages, shredded by the comments of the headmaster who talked and talked, the boy looked at the pages and the anger welled up inside him. It certainly would be nice to wad up the pages, make a big ball and stuff it into Gísli, deep into his throat, that dark tunnel. There's no need to vaunt yourself on compliments from me, pride is poison, said Gísli, his voice suddenly prickly. Compliments!, exclaimed the boy, breaking into a smile without realizing it, his eyes still on the marked-up pages;

compliments, he repeated, because it's called a compliment to tear apart a work into which you've put your all, your heart, lungs, breath. The boy looks in astonishment at Kolbeinn, sitting right next to him, his eyes closed, as if sleeping, though with his left ear turned toward them, catching every word. Yes, said Gísli, I call it a compliment to say that you've done quite a good job of this, in some places very finely done indeed, absolutely extraordinary for an uneducated person, I would call that a compliment, wouldn't you call that a compliment from me, Kolbeinn?, he raised his voice, looked over at the skipper, who said nothing, displayed no reaction; absolutely right, muttered Gísli, you're not here, what a wonderful talent to be able to vanish like that, a rare talent, you should give me lessons. I didn't hear it, the compliment, I mean, said the boy apologetically, I just saw that you'd marked up everything, thought that it was no good. Is that so, did you think that? Yes. But what was that smile of yours supposed to mean, then? I was just thinking. Thinking about what, what was so amusing? Well, said the boy, embarrassed, that it would be fun to stuff the pages down your throat, at which Kolbeinn laughed, or at least emitted a noise like an old, grouchy dog that finds something amusing, entirely unexpectedly: a nice piece of meat, an extinguished sex drive.

And the boy reads these pages, had managed to rewrite them in time, followed Gísli's suggestions, corrections, for the most part, reads them as the rain pounds the world, pounds the house, pounds the horses and the wind tears up the sea. He reads and tries to forget that right now the sea is breaching the embankments, flooding the earth in heavy torrents, and to top it off there's this gale, as if to punish us for having enjoyed the light, the gentleness of summer.

There's power in this text, says Helga after the boy has read the five pages, these words that he found in the language and used for bridge-building so that others, as well as he himself, could seek out remote worlds, seek out life, feelings, seek out what exists in the distance but of which we weren't aware. Translations, Gísli had said, it's hardly possible to describe their importance. They enrich and broaden us, help us to understand the world better, understand ourselves. A nation that translates little, focusing only on its own thoughts, is constricted, and if it boasts a large population it becomes dangerous to others, as well, because most things are alien to it but its own thoughts and customs. Translations broaden people, and therewith the world. They help you understand distant nations. People hate less, or fear less, what they understand. Understanding can save people from themselves. Generals have a harder time getting you to kill if you have understanding. Hatred and prejudice, I declare to you, are fear and ignorance; you may write that down.

He did so, wrote it all down, then went up to his room and corrected the translation, and has now read it over; he read it as the storm pounded the house, the rain lashed the Village, the horses, the sheep, the earth, and turned the June light to dusk. He concludes his reading, there's power in this text, says Helga; yes, says Geirþrúður, yes, there's power, and she looks at the boy. Even Kolbeinn seems to hem something that can possibly be interpreted as a compliment, that curmudgeon who still hasn't let the boy into his room to view his library, four-hundred books, let alone loan him any, and although the boy hopes for a change every single day, he would never imagine asking, out of the blue, never in his life, a man has his pride. He sits there in the parlour, having accomplished something. Done what's important, something besides pull fish from the deep, dig up peat, stack hay in the barn, and now, while the sky quakes with the storm and ships fight against death, the boy feels as if he matters. He who's been called a variety of names ever since his father drowned ten or twelve years ago, who forgets everything, remembers nothing, hardly notices anything, forgets and loses things. You would have lost it a long time ago, said the old women on the farm where he grew up after everyone died that was supposed to have lived, you would have lost it ages ago, that thing hanging between your thighs, if it wasn't attached to you. He's been called an idiot, an imbecile, a mutton-head, a lout, a plonker, a milksop, a wastrel, a wimp, a scoundrel, a poltroon, scum, and loafer, the language is rich with such words, it's also easy to scold and humiliate, it takes neither talent nor intelligence, let alone courage. But it could be undeniably difficult at times to believe that a physically fit urchin, later an adolescent and young man, could take so long with some chores, could hardly remember anything that his hands were supposed to learn; he might have learned to tie a knot in the evening, and then came night and when he woke his hands had completely forgotten how to tie it. Chances are you're just a dolt, an old woman said to him once, not out of malice, but rather, astonishment. Yet now he's been complimented, which is no small thing for one who's been called many difficult names throughout his life; words have influence, they can sink into you and leave marks, get a person to believe various things about himself; to receive such a compliment, and from these women—the boy is quite close to sobbing. Another five pages in a week, can you manage it?, asks Geirþrúður, raising her wine glass to her lips, those lips that were kissed today, and that kissed; then she was alive, in the deserted valley, she existed, she burned, the birds were startled and the mountains took note of her. Yes, says the boy, convinced, confident, happy, I can manage it, there's zeal in his eyes, while outside the storm rages and the world trembles. It would probably be safer to tie it down so that it doesn't blow out into the darkness of space. Andrea lies in her bed in her basement room and listens to the storm, it's not her bed, admittedly, but Geirþrúður's, as is the entire house, she lies there and can't sleep, tosses and turns, doesn't know how she should lie, how she should live, the wind pounds the house, tears up the sea, which is dark and heavy and restless, even the Lagoon, which is usually still even when breakers beat outside it, is tumultuous and J. Andersen's ship rolls upon it frighteningly, its hold empty.

Lúlli and Oddur had worked tirelessly, along with others, to empty the ship's hold of sacks, bags, barrels, and they succeeded, continual work, many hands, things are often urgent here between the mountains, life is in a rush, or, better put, people, not life itself, which simply exists, is just there, like a flower, like music, like a dagger, like sleet, an abyss, healing light. But whatever life is, extraordinary or commonplace, it was urgent that Andersen's ship, the *St. Louise*, be undocked. Saint Louise. We don't know why she was made a saint, this Louise whom the ship is named after, why she deserved it, what torments she had to suffer, does a person have to suffer torments to deserve the name of saint; can't she be happy, isn't it difficult enough in this world, beautiful enough, noble enough? But it was urgent that *St. Louise* be moved from the pier, another ship was waiting on the Lagoon, heavy with salt, salt is needed to cure the fish, and *Louise* needed to be unloaded in haste, yes, now the men had an opportunity to show what they were made of, work like devils and never quit; if their hands dropped off them with fatigue, they should just screw them back on. The foreman, Kjartan, was in his element, he's a great shouter, great at goading men, sometimes they work at night, even until morning, and if someone grumbles, wants to go home, it's very well, do as you please, but you won't be needing to return anytime soon. Skúli has written pointed articles in opposition to this labour-fervency, an energetic man, that Skúli, not quite an adept in style, his sentences aren't daggers, but rather, hefty cudgels. It's amusing that Skúli should stand up to these devils, but it's not a whit amusing to lose one's job, to fall out of favour; then it's a struggle to survive—are you supposed to watch your children starve in the summer, drop dead from cold in the winter; no?, then, unfortunately, it's better to swallow it all and work, labour on as you're ordered. And the *St. Louise* was emptied of everything that foreign countries have: figs, Aquavit, cotton, planed choice timber, coffee; there were even crates of apples. Oddur dexterously managed to open one without being seen, stuck two apples beneath his coat, and now, as the storm tears apart the June light, howls over the houses and makes the mountains rumble, the three of them sit there, Oddur, Rakel, and Lúlli, at Oddur and Lúlli's, they've sliced the apple and slowly eat this fruit that has drunk in the sunshine and tenderness of faraway worlds. Rakel smiles; dear God, how delightful it is to see her smile in close-up, as the storm shakes this little house furiously, the world has turned into one continuous howl. Whence comes this savage power, now, when the month of June should be plover song over our existence?

Oddur had stopped in to see Rakel towards evening, after they'd finished unloading *Louise*; we saw what was in the offing, the darkening clouds, rising wind, a rumble or two from the mountains, as if it were too much for them to restrain their suppressed wrath. Oddur wanted her to join them, what with a storm in the wings, well, or at least foul weather, and he also had a little something that he and Lúlli wanted to share with her; nor is there any need for you to be alone in such foul weather. But she's often been alone in foul weather, malicious winter storms and she's never been afraid, the only storm that she fears is the one in people; to be more precise, in men, which is worse, infinitely worse, when it's not enough to dress warmly, take shelter, it penetrates you and fills you with anxiety, fear, fills your blood with a maddening drone. Yet Rakel said nothing, of course, about the storms in men; she said, stormy weather is just wind in a hurry, there's little to fear. Still, said Oddur, it would be nice to have you visit, and she went with him, without having meant to, without having dared to, something inside her made the decision and Gísli watched her leave with Oddur, saw how they walked side-by-side. Well, now I'll lose her, he thought, she'll leave the basement and then there'll be nothing more between me and the devil, perhaps I should rent you the basement, he said to his walking stick, which was leaning against the wall by the door and naturally has no mouth, no eyes, no heart; it doesn't matter if you give it a name, names don't change death into life. But the three of them, Oddur, Rakel, Lúlli, eat apples and she smiles and Oddur's heart takes many an extra beat, while out on the Lagoon, *St. Louise* rolls horribly.

——

Inner World

(sonnet wreath)

LÁSZLÓ SÁRKÖZI

László Sárközi was born in Hungary in 1969 and honed his formal poetry skills in a mentorship with the late great Hungarian writer György Faludy (*My Happy Days in Hell*). The sequence of poems presented here form a "sonnet wreath" of fifteen sonnets. The first line of each sonnet begins with the last line of the previous one, so the first fourteen sonnets are woven together like a funeral wreath. Following these, the final sonnet is a "master sonnet," comprising all these fourteen first lines, in order. This form gains especial power from the subject matter. The poet feels the bitter pull of a dual Hungarian/Roma identity—almost a pulling apart—and the classical discipline applied to it, paradoxically, unleashes this beautiful, albeit hard, exposition, just enough to share the record of it with us.

Translated from Hungarian by Andrew Singer.

I. Night

I walk the valley of green and silent dreams
and still don't know where I will be tomorrow;
my moods propel me, they drive me far,
anticipating night, craving respite.

Nightfall is a scaly wound, and then
night's well holds the moon—a brave warrior's fate
in shining armour; recoiling to die again.

Down endless streets, new streets run
and where this movement ends, I've no idea.
I straddle the border-stone, gazing at naught.

Cold flash, and a yellow lamp regards me,
light glints off blue-musted cobblestones:
with ten thousand solitudes, the night caresses,
where a black moon renders every shadow brown.

II. Beggar's sonnet

Where a black moon renders every shadow brown,
from a dirty cardboard box a beggar coughs,
his dog poking him—"Leave me, it still hurts so . . ."—
and eyeing his master in a Faithful Zen Ring.
The dwarf shifts cannily; no-one cares;
he's crawling now on backward-facing knees;
now he throws his cup pugnaciously down:
dawn's anger recoils on marble walls.
So I wandered by with pocketed hands
and spat in the beggar's jolting cup—
may the rest be veiled and then forgotten . . .
but neither of us turned lighter from it.
I'm wretched: good intention has died in me.
My twenty-nine years are just a giddy game.

III. Facing eternity

My twenty-nine years are just a giddy game;
one day I am ornate, the next I'm plain,
an endless whirl of good and bad design.

My life is like a dream—it comes to naught,
realizing absurdly the weight of the grave—
nor is the stone's perfume enjoyed in moss.

Whatever I build is in vain, for windmills
and dusty lips are rumbling from the past,
for all is fleeting that once was joy:
the once-shining diamond shall be as ash.

My light fades, morning falls to night—
once you regaled the evergreen dark
Pandora: a box forever opened, as
I go on—shivering, wounded by light.

IV. Under the Taigetosz

I go on—shivering, wounded by light,
cradling myself like a crying tot,
bled and extruded on a winter's night
to the street, seeing afar with hunted eyes,
and before my eyes the whole future sweeps:
a stepchild—as if a step of fate,
fighting to change, and weary,
     on whom the people trod:
with a debtor's life I am bundled clodwards.
In me the years fly with flaming hair.
What do I seek here? Clumsiness merely;
I see the world uncomprehending and afraid
and knock about further after lost shadows
already known; no one ever misses me
and I invent anew my own small world.

And I invent anew my own small world
I hated—yet I can't transcend my blood;
shame is rotting my heart. Now I proclaim:

my eyes, tear-blackened, shine like a dark moon,
because I am gypsy, because I am Hungarian,
because I wear two swords and my mortal steps
lead to the end, smouldering unto ash.

Anywhere at all waits the other: a problem-sea;
in secret, under grass, old animal cravings
offend his virtue, stabbing with pitchfork eyes!

My drops of strength evaporate, only small dreams
sustain me, and blades cut into flesh;
my homeland is foreign, it would clip my weak wings:
free will and desire: to live, like seagulls . . . .

László Sárközi

VI. Me

Free will and desire: to live, like seagulls,
forever . . . people don't see! The whirlpool pulls,
I must adapt, yet my downfall is a given law.
(Will I manage later to die like a Samurai?)

One morn in the dust of a run-down cement plant
I found poetry; there above the sky
little hills sang—every flower became
my sweet prison, and I grasped Humanity no more.

A new feeling-world circulated in me:
and like a sword-blade, proud-grey, there shines
a wine-brown verse on deliquescent walls.

I craved light—I went between the clouds,
but I was not led by brain, nor by Man;
rather it is passion which follows me down.

VII. Drunken sonnet

Rather it is passion which follows me down;
—true, I didn't frolic, for I was drunk and dizzy,
the pint's handle propped me night and morn,

then the horizon darkened before me
& I would have set out, Ulysses to Ithaca,
if I didn't fear my tired legs at night
would give out under me: at last I crawl away . . .

hating: what a horrid stinking glop slumps along?
Sloth: are you human? I don't ask anymore
if it's an animal, this almost-human sin!

As if it's just snowed, that's how that night fell;
I tripped, and a bush set on me. Thus I live:
harsh winter pervades even the autumn in me.

László Sárközi

VIII. In the grip of time

Harsh winter pervades even the autumn in me.
A thousandth of a second's an eternity
like the downpour trashing my rotting cross.

The lead hand shuffles, hours beckon minutes;
plague eats away a thoughtful bachelor
as he passes on his curved walking stick.

Time, kind enemy, ripens and passes.
My dream sifts like dust, and falls on my dust
judgmental, and wind scatters the lost time.

Suffering-become-ash that once had substance,
there will never be one to keep track
of all the timeless time crammed into graves.

And I didn't notice how long I'd drifted;
my path—a faded crow now—thrones my head.

My path—a faded crow now—thrones my head
and I hate autumn's big, colorful death
and I fear the strutting-peacock life
I look back onto—posing, feather-spread:

denying beauty, like a conniving icon
that loves itself, gazes, and slaps its face;
I'm a dark-walker on my chessboard fate:
someone else moves me, till I reach the box;
I dreamed a dragon flying in azure sky—
and a lamb-cloud's blood fell into the Jordan.

My troubled soul's on fire, unfathoming,
(like a person who never changes:
hates terribly, and dreams with fear)
while my heart worships its muse once again.

X. Poetry

While my heart worships its muse once again
a mud-island rises from a deeply troubled lake . . .

Past, present, or future? It's all one in the end;
I live in my own time, denying everything.

What is poetry without being? Material!
And being without poetry—material unformed.

Like one touched by the seven fingers of hell;
his faith is lost, it never does return.

I heard the silent word, with eyes enflamed,
and like reality, it did strike my fancy:

that the Lord is mighty, and I think defenseless,
rather only my rotten soul is endless.

And in my adult gene-helix lives the child,
the Body and Soul Universe of Poetry.

XI. Shards

The Body and Soul Universe of Poetry
is like my fallen childhood. In my head
my good teacher's warning rings: "Wherever
you go, my boy, water turns to fire as you pass."

Since I was baking carrots with another
at the bottom of the haystack; burned
both clothes and haystack—there goes my pocket-money
—my buddy got it (he slaps his pocket proudly);

at night I stole money from his pajamas,
replaced with spices. Thus I tottered around
the morning, and how he woke—spying his long face . . .
I had to kneel in the corner all day on corn . . .

I was a child, and many problems gathered . . .
I'm young, my life has been but fancy . . .

(for János Bogdán)

XII. In the pull of antagonisms

I'm young, my life has been but fancy,
what a hated peasant, alien and stray,
a flung-out frozen splotch of standing snow.

The Hungarian gets sloshed and my thoughts
bode ill—worries churn—being and transience—
I'd drink, though my worker-self won't allow good wine—
swill-blinded, I stomached it, and it was fine.

Thus I barely lived, knowing this country's a carcass-well—
imbalance is the Hungarian pain-foible
behind which, the deeply-rubbed spine of truth—

I don't know who pushed on what—new will,
duties—then misery, self-knowledge, zeal—
whatever—my soul-pair wants to while away—
and I wait for night-darkness, somewhere among oaks.

And I wait for night-darkness, somewhere among oaks
by a grave sunk in the earth, one plodding butterfly
framing the flower garden. This silence is welling,
but comfort not even a crypt-silence can give

—live creeping ivy rustles over every brick
—and on the slanted wall, wind whistles through cracks:
an iron angel with lung trouble, puking blood.

Here's where we've come to, suave speech fallen cold.
You'd call, but work awaits you elsewhere
and your eyes don't see your body's blotches
and no more cleave to the red line

of your once so soft and luscious lips,
like the earth's selfish kiss later answered
mutely, like large dreams witnessing the moon.

László Sárközi

XIV. Civilization

Mutely, like large dreams witnessing the moon:
flowers hardly live here, the world's packed it in;
you realize too late what your life foretold:

your life—false heaven! or thundering hell!
no rose bush stands above all loves;
in "sentimental" winds, industrial gases churn:

it turns the nose and gut, lungs breathe it in—
my rotting brain screams! I start to think:
like a Neanderthal on whose face
appears by chance the twist of rationality:

Chaos! and we proudly become brain-beings!
. . . that I fly from all this, forever and far.
I've sought my tiny home forever because—
resigned—I'm already seeking my own calm:
I walk the valley of green and silent dreams.

Master Sonnet

I walk the valley of green and silent dreams
where a black moon renders every shadow brown.
My twenty-nine years are just a giddy game.

I go on—shivering, wounded by light,
and I invent anew my own small world;
free will and desire: to live, like seagulls,
rather it is passion which follows me down.

Harsh winter pervades even the autumn in me,
my path—a faded crow now—thrones my head,
while my heart worships its muse once again;
the Body and Soul Universe of Poetry.

I'm young, my life has been but fancy,
and I wait for night-darkness, somewhere among oaks
mutely, like large dreams witnessing the moon.

———

László Sárközi

The Brahmadells:
A North Atlantic Chronicle
(novel excerpt)

JÓANES NIELSEN

Jóanes Nielsen, born in 1953, is one of the most popular authors in the Faroe Islands. He has published three novels, eight collections of poetry, two plays, and several short stories and essays. He has been nominated for the Nordic Literature Prize for the fifth time with this novel.

The Brahmadells is a history of two families on the Faroe Islands from the middle of the eighteenth century through today. Durita Dahl Djurhuus from the *Guardian* explains, "What makes Faroese so unique is that the population speaking it is so small and the language has been isolated for hundreds of years. Faroese is very close to the Old Norse, so some ancient sounds are preserved in the language just as others are in Icelandic. Every town has its own dialect."

Original is in Faroese; translation by Kerri Pierce.

The 185th Birthday

Eigil Tvibur closed the cemetery gate behind him and, as often happened when he stepped into the great oaks' shadow, his mind grew calm. The trees were among the city's oldest living inhabitants; thanks to their age and beauty, they were treated with the greatest respect.

When the municipality first installed drainpipes and laid sidewalks along Dr. Jakobsensgøtu in the sixties, it was necessary to move the south stone wall somewhat farther in. That meant that two of the trees came to stand just outside the cemetery; in order to protect them, attractive iron grills were placed around the trunks.

The spruces farther up the yard were also a pleasure to behold. A hundred years ago, Gerd, who married the tradesman Obram from Oyndarfjørður, brought some root cuttings back to the Faroes in a tub. She had been visiting her family in Bergen, and the tub spent the entire trip securely fastened to the ship's deck. Perhaps the act of defying storms from heaven and sea had implanted something joyful and proud in the trees' souls. Whatever the case, Eigil had the feeling that one bright day the trees would burst out singing: *Yes, we love this land . . .*

The rowanberry trees were scrawny and grew best on the cemetery's west side, although some had also been planted outside of it. Indeed, a true vogue for experimentation had swept that part of Tórshavn right before World War I. The trees had grown quickly, and the beautiful crowns with their conspicuous light green leaves provided pleasure to almost five generations of west city inhabitants, not to mention to the countless starlings and sparrows that had sat and whistled or chirped in the branches throughout the years. Now the trees had stopped growing, that much was obvious from the uppermost branches, which were leafless, barkless, and broke off easily. Light green and reddish carpets of moss grew up the trunks, and when the sun was shining, golden beams of light seeped through the loosely woven crowns. Actually, the trees were coming to resemble the people over which they watched. And there was nothing strange about that. The roots, after all, had long been imbibing bodily fluids; eventually, one becomes what one drinks.

The gravel crunched under the soles of his boots, and when Eigil reached the graves of the nameless children, he stopped like he always did. He knew nothing of their history. Presumably, they were stillborns or newborns taken by some sudden, devastating death. The graves looked exactly like the zinc tubs in which women used to wash clothes. However, they had no bottoms. They also had no cross at their heads, and the tubs were upturned on the grass. In the months of June and July, buttercups and orchids grew out of the holes in the tubs; their stalks waved yellow and reddish-blue summer flags.

Eigil continued to the grave of former country surgeon Napoleon Nolsøe. At one time, his dislike of the man had been so great that on New Year's Eve 1980 he had dishonored Nolsøe's grave. He had been convinced that Napoleon Nolsøe was the prototypically devious Faroese nationalist and that, because of him, nationalism's cultural aspect in particular had become an epidemic.

If only he had kept his mouth shut about his grave defiling, nothing more would have happened!

However, in December 1992, when Eigil was up for re-election on Tórshavn's city council, his misdeed was aired by the newspaper *Sosialurin*. The man who had represented the Independence Party on the city council for four years was hung out as a gravepisser! The newspaper wrote that he had disgraced an honorable man's grave in the same way as had the Nazis and anti-Semites when they painted or sprayed their slogans across Jewish graves. Or worse even: Whereas the anti-Semites' paint came from cans and so could be considered impersonal, urine originated in a warm, autonomous body.

With only the light from the bracket lamp in the hallway, when he stood and spoke into the floor-length mirror, he had defended himself by saying that the action was inspired by the man of letters, Ole Jacobsen. In volume 6 of *Fra Færørerne—Úr Føroyum*, which the Danish-Faroese Society published in 1971, and which Ole Jacobsen edited, the author succeeded in convincing the reader, or at least Eigil Tvibur, that in 1846 Napoleon Nolsøe had broken the Hippocratic Oath. That accusation was not just hard; it was enough to destroy a man's legacy.

In 1846, namely, measles was ravaging the Faroes; in Tórshavn alone around 50 of the 800 inhabitants died. Dr. Napoleon, who at that time practiced in Nólsoyarstova, was asked by county administrator Pløyen to travel to Suðuroy to help with the crisis. He would be paid 50 *rigsdaler* a month. However, Napoleon refused to depart.

A few years after Eigil read Ole Jacobsen's article, the literary history *Bókmentasøga I* by Árni Dahl was published. It was clear that Dahl greatly respected the doctor. Indeed, page 75 of the book featured a large photograph of the man; the picture was accompanied by a short biography, and Dahl reprinted a few snippets composed in Faroese by Cand. med. & chir. N. Nolsøe.

That made Eigil furious. He had always been disgusted by the type of nationalist who claimed to love the native poetry but couldn't care less about the country's inhabitants. As Regin Dahl wrote: "I love the land, hate the people." Or maybe it was the reverse. Eigil simply had no tolerance for that kind of verbiage. And that was more or less how Napoleon Nolsøe was described in Ole Jacobsen's essay. He loved the Faroese songs and ballads, but in 1846 had turned his back on his dying countrymen.

If Eigil had his way, such a man as Napoleon Nolsøe would never appear in Faroese literary history. He simply had no place there. Not that he was against giving authorial villains their due in histories or reference works or even naming streets and ships after them. Not at all. One of his great skaldic heroes was the Nazi sympathizer Knut Hamsun. And without authors such as the Marquis de Sade, Céline, and Jean Genet, the French literary mouth would lose much of its bite.

But Dr. Napoleon was no Genet, and he had done nothing worthy of literary acclaim.

Sure, he might have contributed to the development of Faroese orthographic rules, but that was about it. Otherwise, the man had recorded songs and ballads, but had not actually composed anything himself, and what he did write down had already been collected and documented by others. All he had done was transcribe transcripts, that was his achievement, and to fill literary history with transcribers would be both unfitting and ridiculous.

At an Authors' Society meeting, Eigil declared that the names that appeared in literary history were just as randomly chosen as the names on the society's membership roster. One man belonged because he had translated two or three minimalistic children's books some twenty-five years back. Another had taken part in a short story contest launched by well-meaning pedagogues just as many years ago, and the result had been some purely sentimental, pedagogical drivel! And a third might have edited a festschrift for some alcoholic sleepwalker in the Academy. Such was the society's membership roster—at least for the most part. The few authors who actually deserved to be there had been branded "cultural mafia" by the media.

The danger here was that when another Árni Dahl decided to write a new literary history in half a century or so, that the person would turn to the Society's membership roster in search of fitting representatives. People who were no doubt skilled with a copy machine would be called notable bearers of Faroese culture.

Eigil could see only one reason that Dr. Napoleon was honored with a place among the Faroese full and half gods. He had the right DNA profile! The doctor was the son of the old business manager Jákup Nolsøe, and therefore the nephew of poet and national icon, Nólsoyar-Páll. It was solely for that reason that Árni Dahl had smuggled him in through the back door of his literary history!

When Eigil reached Napoleon's grave, he set down his bag. It was August 26th, exactly one hundred and eighty-five years since Napoleon was born. Eigil placed a hand on the stone and wished him happy birthday; as so often before, he also asked Napoleon's forgiveness for having sullied his sleeping bones.

On the other side of the cemetery path was a concrete basin with a tap. He ran some water into a bowl, screwed the lid off the container of stone cleaner, and poured in the strong stuff. He did not immediately notice when some of it splashed onto his coat sleeve; when he finally saw the spot, it did not make much of an impression. Truthfully, it fit his overall appearance. He had not washed or shaved in several days, and his bright brown eyes sought the source of every small sound, be it a rustle in the newly fallen leaves or a bird suddenly bursting into song. Compared to his body, his head was strikingly small; he was quite large, and the grimy coat made him look even more massive.

Eigil's original plan had been to clean the entire stone, and also to scrape off the moss and the lichen, but that would only make the stone dirtier. Indeed, the patina would certainly vanish. He knelt down before the gravestone and, with a small screwdriver, began cleaning the engraved lettering of the accumulated debris. And there were 132 letters in total. Eigil had plenty of time, however, and when he finished his cleaning, he took a paintbrush from his bag and began to brush and wash each individual letter with stone cleaner.

Just like a scoured corpse, Eigil thought, and a giggle broke through his lips. Exactly—a scoured corpse. Like a skeleton preserved in dry skins, or as Eliot wrote of the whispering voices:

Quiet and meaningless
As wind in dry grass
Or rats' feet over broken glass
In our dry cellar.

Calm, hr. Eigil, calm, he told himself.

A rose branch twisted around the marble plate. It had been finely etched into the gray material and the concave leaves sported some soft moss.

With a smile he asked himself whether or not it would have bothered Napoleon Nolsøe that Nils Tvibur's great grandson was sitting here painting these letters with silver-bronze.

Eigil and Karin had planned to drink a birthday toast at the gravesite, and his bag contained a bottle of Chablis and two glasses. He uncorked the bottle, lit a cigarette, and considered the newly painted letters:

HERE LIES BURIED

RETIRED COUNTRY SURGEON

NAPOLEON NOLSØE

MARCH 3RD 1878

THIS STONE ERECTED

BY HIS FRIENDS IN REMEMBRANCE

OF WHAT HE MEANT TO THEM

DURING HIS DAY.

Karin, however, had not come. They had agreed that she would be here at four o'clock, and now it was nearly half past five.

He blew tobacco from his lips, he was a clumsy smoker, but it calmed him to have a cigarette between his fingers.

Could the situation be so fucking awful that he had actually wounded her?

His mind turned to the Dusty Springfield song, "You Don't Have to Say You Love Me." He had played it again and again during the blissful week they had spent together.

Suddenly, it occurred to Eigil that perhaps they had never even made a date, or that perhaps it existed only in his mind. He had intended to invite her to eat at the newly opened restaurant in Nólsoyarstova. The building had been Napoleon Nolsøe's childhood home. Later, he had kept his medical consultation there, and when he married Henriette Løbner in 1874, she had moved in as well.

The perfect setting for a cozy meal!

Could all the hell he was catching from the Independence Party have destroyed that plan? There was something here that did not fit.

Eigil felt his hand shake as he poured wine into his glass, and when he glanced toward the gate, he dropped the glass altogether.

There stood his mother. The face of the person closest to him in the world was far too anxious, and her hands gripped each other, as if she were afraid to lose them. At her side were two policemen.

The Orange

The passenger sprang from the cutter. Like a sail his coat spread out around him, and while he hung in the air with both arms outstretched he looked just like a bird.

The sight was neither unusual nor ridiculous, but Tóvó still covered his mouth, biting his fingers to keep from bursting into uncontrollable laughter. On board the cutter were three travel trunks, each holding medicine and various instruments meant for minor surgeries: scalpels, scissors, amputation saws, and a copious amount of gauze. Also, alcohol, camphor, laxatives, quinine, opium drops, and mercury ointment.

Farther out lay the three-masted schooner *Havfruen*. They had had a good wind from Copenhagen. The first day they beat to windward, but after they were free of Skagerrak, the wind blew from the south and southeast. For seven days they traveled with full sails, and at midnight they dropped anchor at Tórshavn's harbor.

Finally, the trunks were unloaded and the passenger turned to Tóvó. At that, the amusement left the boy's eyes; the passenger saw that this laughter-prone person was a six-year-old who had come out to Vippan to watch. The passenger's gaze was friendly, albeit searching. He took an orange from his coat pocket and handed the boy the odd reddish-yellow object. Tóvó didn't know Danish, but he understood enough to know that an *orange* was something you could eat.

Manicus and Panum

It had been only two weeks since the newspapers in the Danish capital had published an account of the measles epidemic ravaging the Faroe Islands.

The article first appeared in *Fædrelandet* on June 17, 1846, and even though it was uncredited, one could guess that Dr. Napoleon was the author; or that, inspired by Dr. Napoleon, it had been written by Niels C. Winther, or Doffa, as his friends called him. *Berlingske Tidende* reprinted the article and the news was deemed so alarming that the Rentekammer immediately sought to send medical aid to the Faroes. Two doctors were asked to take on the task.

One was twenty-six-year-old August Manicus. His father, Claus Manicus, had been country surgeon on the Faroe Islands from 1820 to 1828. Accordingly, his son had spent his childhood in Tórshavn and had been a playmate of both Vencil Hammershaimb and Doffa.

The second doctor, the orange man, was better known as Peter Ludvig Panum.

For five months, the two traveled the islands administering medical aid. Panum also made a thorough examination of Faroese living conditions. He scrutinized factors such as housing, hygiene, diet, and food preparation— and he recorded every last detail. He also described the clothing, and the overall affect that weather had on the health of body and soul.

His results were published in the doctors' medical journal *Bibliothek for Læger* in the spring of 1847.

Of course, before June 17, 1846, what no one, not even Panum himself, realized was that his treatise would become one of modern epidemiology's great breakthroughs.

Like Panum, Manicus also described his sojourn in the Faroes, and even though his report, which could be read in *Ugeskrift for Læger*, was not as comprehensive as Panum's, he viewed the connection between medical complications and social living conditions with a sharper eye. He writes: "Bøigden Sumbø was one of the sites where the epidemic claimed the most victims. The poverty of its inhabitants, the poor housing conditions, and the fact that all at once measles gripped the larger part of the inadequately nourished population, who were moreover apt to follow any sort of advice, explains this."

Manicus further added that the disease spared nearly all of the Danish families and was markedly milder among the well-to-do natives.

In a footnote to her doctoral thesis "Kunnskap og makt," which was published in 2006, Beinta í Jákupsstovu writes: "The mid-1800s was a period characterized by strong ideological currents; Manicus might have sympathized with political ideas surrounding the promotion of social equality or with Faroese nationalism."

She admits, however, that no extant sources support this idea.

Mogul

Mogul laid his head in Tóvó's lap. He yawned deeply, and when the boy began to pick the pus from his brown eyes, he did not resist; he also swallowed the pusball that the boy rolled between his fingers and placed on his long tongue.

Presumably, the dog realized that Tóvó was the reason he was still alive. He was in his twelfth year, and as sometimes happens with an old dog, he was liable to snap at people. He did the same with other domestic animals, and one day he mauled one of fru Løbner's hens. Now, Martimann said, his days were numbered.

Tóvó was uncertain what having numbered days actually meant. He could count to nineteen, and he knew there was such a thing as "counting the days of Christmas,"[1] but surely that was not what his father was thinking of. However, when Martimann tied up the dog and went for his muzzle-loader, it was clear to the boy that Mogul was going to be shot. That is what it signified to have days numbered.

He burst into tears. He said it was the chicken who had started it all. The bird had given Mogul loads of trouble. It had been sent by the Devil, and at night, when everyone was sleeping, Tóvó was going to set fire to every chicken in town.

His father was astonished at the strength of his son's reaction. He had never seen Tóvó stand there and stomp and shake his fists. The boy was only six, but the way he was carrying on, he resembled a raging dwarf. Tóvó put his arms around Mogul's neck and said that he would never let go.

For a moment, Martimann considered the situation. He knew how much the boy loved the dog, and if he shot it, his son would undoubtedly see him as an enemy for a long time to come.

He could take fru Løbner some fish in exchange for the mauled hen, she would probably accept that. And it was such a sweet picture: Tóvó sobbing with his arms around Mogul's neck, while the dog sat inquiringly on its hind legs.

Martimann loosened the rope, but to show that he still had some authority, he gave the dog a kick that sent it spinning across the yard.

Tóvó continued to cry. He hated his father. Hoped a whale would bite his arm off, or that a stone would come flying through the air and strike him right between the eyes.

---

1   A Faroese dance tradition where a certain number of counting songs or rhymes are sung during the last dance of Shrove Monday.

The Little Wandering Church

Even though it was a regular weekday, Tórshavn was a ghost town and had been that way for several weeks. No hammer stroke was heard between the houses, no women were washing clothes in the river, and no playful children were rolling hoops in the alleyways. The city, which under normal circumstances could man sixteen eight-rowers, could hardly man a single boat in May or June.

From a bird's-eye view, the turf thatched houses resembled giant limpets that had adhered to the rocks and gave no sign of life.

The situation was so dire that the Provost, hr. Hans, bought several barrels of grain with help from the poor relief fund. One pot occupied the stove of Adelheid Debess, the midwife, and the other hung over a hearth belonging to an old married couple on Bakki. Some of the disease-struck were able to retrieve their own soup, but households whose every member lay coughing and vomiting required others to bring them their meals, and in some cases it was also necessary to feed them.

One of the unselfish souls caring for the sick was Old Tóvó. In his younger years he had been known as quite a ladies' man, yet women still let him slip his hand under their necks and lift their heads up while he gave them water or soup to drink. He inhaled their sweet womanly aroma, and a female relation from Bakkahella told him that he had always liked it when women were sick, because they were so compliant. She tried to smile, said he had always been a blowhard.

No one entered the church. Ever since the measles had come to hold sway, the church only opened its doors to the dead. Up to eight coffins at a time stood on trestles in the choir and down the central aisle. According to established protocol in cases of disease, the coffins were tarred within, and the smell of tar and decay filled the church with a perpetual gloom. The dead were taken from their homes as soon as possible, and they were either washed or prepared in some other way before the cart retrieved them. An old tradition dictated that a corpse's big toes be bound together to prevent the dead from walking, but measles had undermined most traditions. And who knew if the dead even wanted to walk again. Why would they? In May and June death in Tórshavn was about as naked as it could get, and to ghost around when autumn storms were shrouding the city in a salt sea fog—that was something one could not bid the living or the dead.

Adelheid dried her tears and smiled. What a bizarre coffin flotilla it must be, she thought, that met out on eternity's waters. The sails were whatever clothes people had been wearing when they died: nightgowns, pants, shawls, and tattered shifts.

Sure, sure, answered her husband, Ludda-Kristjan, and shrugged his left shoulder. He might be one of the volatile souls from Kák, but against his wife there was nothing much he could to do. He dared not tell her to shut her damn mouth and stop all this strange nonsense. However, that's how the flock around Provost Lund talked. They were so sentimental it was outright revolting.

An exception was the Norwegian corporal Nils Tvibur, or Muhammed, as he was also called. On Cross Day at the beginning of May he paid a visit to Ludda-Kristjan's workshop and said there was no point in wasting wood. Considering the circumstances, it was enough to make every coffin a foot high, and if the epidemic continued, they would have to make some other provision.

Ludda-Kristjan asked if he was thinking of a mass grave; that was exactly what Nils had in mind. If a mass grave was dug, they would need to wrap the dead in linen and sprinkle the corpses with lime.

Among the soldiers, also known as "hunters," stationed at Fort Skansin, Nils Tvibur was the one the county administrator most trusted. You could take the corporal at his word; the man meant what he said. The hunters were responsible for unloading the ships that came to trade. In turn, it was trade that funded the operation at Skansin. As corporal, Nils was the obvious choice for foreman. Sometimes he could be hard on people, even his own men, but he was good at getting things done.

His Christian name was Selleg, and he hailed from the peninsula of Sveio in Hordaland. However, no one ever called him Nils Selleg, and he always signed his name "Nils Tvibur" in the Skansin log. He was called Tvibur because he was a twin,[2] and since he had been born last, it was his older twin brother who had acquired the land lease.

And Nils Tvibur was no self-coddler. When the gravedigger succumbed to measles in May, Nils took up his spade, and he also drove the horses that pulled the cart. When the corpses were too large, he broke their necks so that he could nail the lid on the coffin shut.

"Damn," he said one day after hr. Hans had blessed a man from Hoyvík whose neck he had just broken. "He looks like he's listening to something I can't hear. So long as it's not the footfalls of Iblis."

2   Faroese: *tvíburi*, or "twin."

Hr. Hans blanched when he heard the name Iblis. "Don't you go spouting the name of Muslim Satan in a Christian church," he said, making the sign of the cross over the corpse.

"Sure thing," Nils answered.

There were not many days that the corporal and the priest did not cross paths, and one day hr. Hans asked why Nils was so infatuated with the Muslim faith.

Nils responded that faith in general did not really interest him. Neither the Muslim nor the Christian faith, nor Judaism for that matter. But last year a man had died whom he had greatly respected, the editor Henrik Wergeland. Nils said that he had not read his poetry, but the things he had written about religious freedom—those were manly words indeed. It was Wergeland who had opened his eyes to Muhammed, or the great Desert Captain, as Nils tended to call him. Since then he had tried as much as possible to follow the Muslim way of life. He knew that the Muslim people lived next to the high mountain where Noah's ark was stranded, and that their cities spread all the way down to the Persian Gulf. There were also Muslims along the entire North African coast. They were not so close-fisted as to refuse charity to the poor, but they were also fearless warriors.

It was the general state of emergency that prompted hr. Hans to make an unusual decision. Since the church only had room for the dead, he decided to bring hymns and prayers out to his fellow townsfolk.

In the beginning, he walked alone, briefly stopping at Bakkahella, at Doktaragrund, up above the library, or simply whenever he saw a door ajar. He prayed an Our Father, blessed the household, and then sang a verse.

But after Anna Sofie and Henriette Løbner, mother and daughter, joined him, some other poor souls turned out as well. For the most part, they sang "Fare, World, Farewell" by the Danish hymn-writer, Thomas Kingo. They sang it to the sarabande-melody, and their swaying tread gave the group a solemn and peculiar appearance.

No poet has made a greater impact on the Faroese national spirit than Thomas Kingo, and when Professor Christian Matras translated "Fare, World, Farewell" to Faroese in 1929, he walked the same narrow streets as hr. Hans before him, humming to himself, in an effort to instill the unique Kingo-musicality into the verses.

The group also sang the more contemporary and milder hymn by Oehlenschläger, "Teach Me, Oh Wood, to Fade Glad Away," and when they passed the house in Geil, Tóvó sometimes stood in the door and watched and listened to the little wandering church.

Tóvó's Flies

That morning Tóvó was awakened by his mother. She had been up a few times during the last two days, but she did not speak. She was not her usual self, and now that the measles and its aftereffects had lost their grip, she would break into sobs so heartrending that Tóvó had to cover his ears; he went outside, even though it did not help. He had no idea that these crying spells were a burgeoning insanity, and that in the coming years his mother would earn the nickname Crazy Betta.

In *Iagttagelser*, or *Observations*, Panum wrote: "there is hardly any other country, or indeed any metropolis, in which mental diseases are so frequent in proportion to the number of people as on the Faroes."

Tóvó's brother, Lýðar, and his sister, Ebba, were still confined to their bunks, and their grandfather had placed a spittoon on the bench between him. An old household remedy said seawater had curative powers, and therefore grandfather often made the trip to the little promontory of Bursatanga to rinse out the spittoon. He covered it with a lid to keep the flies away, but nonetheless they buzzed around this interesting wooden container. Sometimes they sat on the rim, and while they cleaned their shiny legs, Tóvó struck. Most he killed as soon as he caught them, but some he tortured to death. He would place the prisoner on its back and sense the faint buzzing of the fly body as a tickle against his forefinger and thumb, and before its tiny heart had beat its last, its plucked wings and legs were on the bench. Like a ship with no oarsman a fly would sail around and around the small tin-lined sea. It kept trying to reach the edge, and every time it had almost found purchase with two or three legs, it would be mercilessly shoved away, until eventually it gave up fighting for its wretched life.

In the tobacco tin, which Tóvó had stashed behind the Heegaard stove's lion feet, there were often nineteen dead flies. A piece of twine was wound around the container, and when he took the lid off, it smelled slightly of rot, but mostly of *kardus*. The flies that had not been tortured to death lay with their wings pressed tight against their bodies and their skinny legs curled up, like they were begging forgiveness for their very existence.

Whether tortured, crushed, or drowned, the flies all had one thing in common: they were victims in the war Tóvó single-handedly waged against the measles. From what he understood, measles were a kind of fly, too. One single glance from their itty bitty measles-eyes and people immediately grew feverish and began to cough and rave madly. Some also sang madly, humming words mixed with guttural sounds, until they either gave out and fell asleep or became blue in the face and stopped breathing.

Still, he did not understand why the measles flies had not shot their rays at grandfather, or why Mogul was not affected. On the other hand, the way they behaved, there were a few cows that certainly had the measles.

What they should do was go up to the small lake, Hoyvíkstjørn, and out into the Konmansmýri marsh and eat grass and clover and thyme; their calves could frolic so that they sprang straight into the air. Sometimes the cattle grazed all the way up near Svartafoss, and when Betta and the children went up there to pick berries one sunny day last summer, they saw several white ravens and a heron fishing in the falls.

Svartafoss was not as high a waterfall as Villingardalsfoss, and it was also lower than the streams that cast themselves over the cliffs at Kaldbaksbotn, but Svartafoss was still nicer than any other waterfall. The rocks were black, and when the sun shone they were wonderfully warm to touch and sit on. Small red flowers glinted among the plants that grew along the stream and hung from the rocks, and in the rock crevices you could see bunches of yellow roseroots. Lýðar called the high reeds that grew north of the waterfall "grass knives," and they were so sharp you could cut yourself on them.

Their mother said that rainbows also loved Svartafoss, and her children believed her. It was at Svartafoss that the rainbows' colors were mixed. After that, proud and beautiful, they would straddle the fjord straight across to *Nólsoy*. Sometimes a rainbow would strike Heimistova, where their grandmother and grandfather lived, and sometimes it would reach all the way up to Eystnes on Eysturoy. Svartafoss was pure paradise for all who loved berries, said their mother, drying the red berry juice off their lips. Lýðar lay splashing in the creek, and when he came up again, mother wrapped the naked boy in her shawl.

Now everything was different. There was no one left to milk the cows; they had gone insane and bellowed through people's doors.

Tóvó's concern for Mogul was due to the way he had reacted against his father the day Martimann wanted to kill the dog, but he dared not tell anyone that, not even his grandfather.

However, he did ask his grandfather why he did not get sick.

Old Tóvó answered that, the fact of the matter was, he was half-grown in 1781 when measles had raged the last time, and that you could not have the disease twice. That was also the reason that he was not afraid to visit people and help them. And perhaps the old man sensed that something else was bothering the boy, because he added that dogs whose breath stank could not get the disease either.

Tóvó asked if the disease really did come flying through the air. His grandfather explained that on Annunciation Day a ship had come from Denmark, and that the ship had brought the disease to Tórshavn.

Tóvó had heard of Denmark and he knew that a prince lived down there. He had even seen the prince when he had come to Tórshavn on a warship two years ago. Suddenly, he frowned and asked why the prince would send a ship full of measles-flies to the Faroes?

Old Tóvó suppressed a smile as he looked into this serious and lovable boy's face. He had not been as fond of his own children as he was of Tóvó. And the boy was so quick-thinking. The journey from thought to question took no more time than the blink of an eye. Grandfather knew about all the dead flies Tóvó kept in the tobacco tin, and one day he had watched the boy drown one poor creature in the measuring pot. However, he said nothing, just waited outside until the deed was done.

Now he explained to Tóvó that, of all the castles in the world, the measles castle was the hardest to conquer. Only the cunning prince could sneak through the gate and raise the victory flag.

Grandma Pisan

On Pentecost the cart stopped for the first time in front of the Geil house. Grandfather opened the door and Nils Tvibur and another man came in to retrieve Pisan, or Grandma Pisan, as the children called her.

Pisan was from Hestoy, and when Farmer Támar's oldest son got her pregnant, and she gave birth to a daughter, she took her own child's life.

That's what Old Tóvó told his great grandson several years later.

Pisan gave birth to her daughter in a peat shed up on the island, he said. And the child was healthy. She smelled so freshly of the womb; Pisan could feel the warm breath from the newly developed lungs against her neck and chin. She said the breath from the small nostrils and tiny mouth was like a storm, the strongest she had ever experienced. She put the baby to her breast, and when the child had nursed its fill, Pisan did what plenty other unmarried mothers did during the slave law[3] years—she killed her own child. With the little nape trustfully resting against her hand, she pressed

---

3   Law passed in 1777 that forbid anyone who did not own land from marrying.

her thumb to the baby's throat, and when its breathing had stopped, she wrapped it in the lined shawl on which she had given birth, bundled it tight, and then sank her unbaptized daughter in a small pond south of Fagradalsvatn.

Old Tóvó stroked his great grandson's hand. He could tell him one thing: If the men on the island decided to drain that pond someday, they would find a mass grave of newborns swaddled in lined shawls. Of course, Pisan would answer for her action on the Last Day. But so would the island's lechers. And the Devil give them what they deserved!

In *Saga Hestoyar*, Pastor Viderø writes: "Plenty of tears have been shed here on Hestoy, but God transforms them to the most beautiful rainbow."

Pisan was never able to see the minister's rainbow. Or rather, one might say that, with a freshly knitted shawl, her feet encased in leather shoes and clogs, and with a bundle under her arm, she fled the rainbow over the fjord.

For many years she earned a living on different farms on Suðurstreymoy. After she moved to a garret in the vicinity of Sjarpholið in Tórshavn, she set fish out to dry on Rundingi and, among other things, helped out in houses where women were giving birth.

The nickname *Pisan*, which means "chick," rhymed with the female body part under her shift, and what she could not settle with money, she settled with her nickname-rhyming body part.

Old Tóvó was one of her long-time suitors and friends, and when she grew old, he pitied her and took her home to the Geil house to live. And it was there she was taken by measles.

The cart came for Pisan on the Eve of Pentecost. Little Tóvó was sick with the measles and did not fully comprehend what was happening. He only saw the blue *pisan*-head as they lifted her into the coffin.

It should be added here that Old Tóvó became a widower in 1822. His wife, Ebba, hailed from Venzilsstova in Kaldbak, and they had two children. Their daughter, Gudrun, was usually called Gudda. At eleven years of age she became maid to the Argir hospital's tenant. In 1820 Claus Manicus was appointed country surgeon, and in the years he worked on the Faroes, Gudda served as his housemaid. When the Manicuses moved in 1828, they invited Gudda to come with them to Denmark. She served as their maid for thirteen years and died unexpectedly at the age of forty-nine.

Old Tóvó's son was also called Tóvó. He and his young wife, Annelin, lived in the Geil house. Annelin was pregnant when young Tóvó went down with the *Royndin Fríða*. She gave birth to Betta in 1810. Shortly thereafter,

Annelin married Finnur, who was a farmer in Kirkja on Fugloy, but she left her small daughter, Betta, to be fostered by her first husband's mother and father in Tórshavn.

Sorrow and Rhyme

Sixteen days later the cart again stopped outside the Geil house. To Tóvó's mind, it was as if a stick had been stuck between the wheel spokes; and when he thought back later, it was as if the cart had stood there his whole childhood, digging and hewing itself deeper and deeper to his soul's bottom.

Nils Tvibur and a man in a mask placed the empty coffin on the floor. The mask had a beak with a little dried moss and caraway and horseradish. The smell was supposed to prevent contagion.

The Geil house had gotten so fine. The floorboards were new. Martimann had laid at least half the floor and installed the stove before the measles broke out. The disease's progression had been as expected. His eyes and cheeks swelled up and he lay in bed with a high fever for a week. When he felt better and his cough was somewhat improved, he thought there was no harm in nailing down a floorboard every now and then. There was no one else to do it, and he could not bring himself to ask Old Tóvó. The old man had enjoyed a good reputation in his years as a shoemaker, but as a carpenter he was not worth much. As a result, Martimann got out of bed; progress was made with every board he nailed fast. He saved the widest boards for the area around the door; they were up to eleven inches in length. The floor had been sawed from a piece of driftwood his father had given him, and on a nice day last summer they had dragged the tree stem to Tórshavn and got it up into the boathouse's loft to dry.

It was the short trip down to the boathouse to retrieve the boards that proved too much. Martimann became damp and cold, and when he lay back down on his bunk he fell victim to all the complications Old Tóvó had constantly warned him against, and which strong Martimann simply could not have imagined.

His intestines felt like they had come to life and were writhing like worms in his gut. Sometimes they squirmed up into his throat and made him vomit, or retreated down into his rectum, spraying filth onto the blanket Old Tóvó had placed beneath him.

Old Tóvó tried to coax him to eat; boiled milk was somewhat satisfying and was also good at providing blockage. However, the mites that lived on *skerpikjøt*[4] were said to be even better at stopping diarrhea. The problem was, they had no dried mutton. Out in the storehouse were several dried fish, and also a barrel of salted whale meat.

Martimann had been the anchorman in the Geil house ever since he and Betta had married. Many summers he had sailed with the Scottish sloop *Glen Rose*, and much of that income went to renovating the dilapidated house. He put new pieces of bark on the roof and asked Ludda-Kristjan to build a double window, which he himself installed. The house was set on stony ground, and Martimann built a chimney in the northwest corner. He placed stones on a small piece of ground in front of the chimney, and that is where he set the stove. The smoking parlor was converted into a kitchen, and all the sunlight that streamed in through the new window quite literally heralded brighter days.

The floor was finished, and the plan was to build a kitchen table where Betta could sort clothes and attend to other household tasks. Martimann was a driven soul, and during the years he lived in the Geil house, there was no dearth.

By New Year's, however, there was not much money left and Old Tóvó could hardly go to country surgeon Regenburg or Dr. Napoleon empty-handed and ask them to come and see to Martimann.

Nonetheless, Old Tóvó spoke to Napoleon, and the doctor told him that dedicated care was about the best they could do for the disease's complications. "I know what I'm talking about," Napoleon said. "Good wishes and constant care, there isn't much more in our power."

Old Tóvó assumed an educated man would not think much of household remedies, and he could not bring himself to ask the doctor for any *skerpikjøt* mites.

As it was, he felt he had no other choice than to do what the city's inhabitants did when the German privateer "Baron von Hompesch" plundered Tórshavn's trade coffers: go out and beg.

The farmers on Húsagarður had meat, but knocking on a Sunman's door, hat in hand—that was not something he could face.

However, Old Tóvó swallowed his shame and made the trip to Quillinsgarður to the former county administrator's wife Anna Sofie von Løbner. He stood in the doorway, and for a moment, while she tapped her knuckles with her fingers, she looked at him in surprise.

---

4   A well-aged, wind-dried mutton that is a specialty of the Faroe Islands.

Old Tóvó could well remember when Anna Sofie was one of Húsagarðbonden's milkmaids. Her father was a cooper, so she was known as Cooper's Anna Sofie. She was a shapely woman, and thanks to her plump figure, she was asked to play one of the maids in Holberg's comedy *The Lying-In Room*.

However, letters were not Anna Sofie's strong suit, she needed someone else to read her lines aloud, at which point she would memorize them. And that other person was no less than Commandant Emilius von Løbner. He was patient and kind and read well, and he never forgot to light a fire in the Bilegger stove so that the room was cozy. Sometimes these readings lasted past midnight, and during the breaks Løbner offered the budding actress sweet wine and fair words. And she let herself be enticed by his ripe charms, becoming giggly, inviting, and compliant.

"Just call me Emilius," he said, placing a sweetmeat on her moist, pink tongue. He received permission to bathe her with an expensive soap, telling her that this was how the illustrious enjoyed themselves in the King's city. He placed a dish of warm water on the table and rubbed soap into the wet washcloth; she consented to let him wash her face and neck and along her hairline. Nor did she protest when he untied her blouse, washed under her arms, and carefully dried the sweat off her heavy breasts. She enjoyed this intriguing midnight game, allowed him suckle her breasts, and made no objection when he undid her skirt. He said "hopsasa," and she lifted her rump while he spread a towel on the chair to keep the plush dry, and the towel was so large that he also folded it over her thatch, so that she would not feel too exposed. While he washed her toes, one after the other, he caressed and patted her thighs, which he called love's white columns. And Anna Sofie purred with well-being, just like the Bilegger stove.

"Just sigh," he whispered. There was no harm in sighing out loud when one felt good.

By the time the comedy played in Fútastova in September 1813, Anna Sofie was pregnant. The couple married in January 1814, the same day Frederik VII signed his name to the document separating Norway from Denmark. In April, Anna Sofie delivered a stillborn male child. Three years later she was pregnant again. She gave birth to Ludvig, named after his Danish grandfather. In 1825, Henriette Elisabeth, named after both her Danish grandmother and her Faroese grandmother, was born.

The reason Løbner left the Faroes the same year that his daughter was born is still a mystery. By that time he was nearly sixty and his health was poor. In particular, his sight was failing, and he often said that his eyes could not tolerate the raw Faroese climate.

There had also been complaints about the way he carried out his office, but precisely how serious these were, no one knows for sure. In the second volume of *Havnar søgu*, Jens Pauli Nolsøe and Kári Jespersen try to shed some light on the man: "To his credit, he compiled Løbner's *Tabellir* in 1813. They form a valuable description of Faroese society and are actually the only precise documentation of the economic conditions in Faroese rural society. For Tórshavn, it was important that he (Løbner) allowed Álaker field to be added to the city in 1807, which nearly doubled the area then belonging to Tórshavn."

However, much about his life remains in the dark, and perhaps for this very reason a number of Løbner's descendants have tried to mystify the man. Among other things, it has been suggested that the insane monarch Christian VII was his father; in that case, Løbner's mother became pregnant when Christian was still a prince. Løbner was born in 1766, the same year that Christian was crowned, and it is not unthinkable that the prince paid a visit to his relations at Augustenborg Palace the year previous. Løbner's father, namely, was chamber lackey at Augustenborg.

It is also difficult to find information on what exactly Løbner did during those last years after he returned to his homeland. There is some indication that he lived with Caroline Wroblewsky, who ran a private school in Copenhagen for a while. Wroblewsky adopted a young girl, Emilie Christine, and she took over her foster mother's school in 1858. Among other things, the *Dansk Kvindebiografisk Leksikon*, a biographical encyclopedia of Danish women, records that: "In 1850 she (Emilie Christine) changed her name to Løbner after her adoptive father, the former county administrator of the Faroe Islands Emilius Marius Løbner, who died the previous year."

What is nonetheless certain is that Løbner spent a quarter of a century on the Faroes, and that he was around sixty when he left. One reason for this lengthy sojourn was the major changes occasioned by the Napoleonic Wars. Denmark, namely, had not waged war since the Great Northern War ended in 1720, and during the long stretch of time that followed, which historians term the "Florissante Period," Copenhagen was transformed into a European trading center. Throughout the various wars that plagued Europe, the Danes sailed the seas under a flag of neutrality, which proved extremely profitable for both ships and maritime trading companies. The Danish-Norwegian trade fleet was the second largest in Europe, and aside from overseeing Danish colonial interests, the fleet sailed the globe, shipping goods out and carrying goods home.

The Florissante Period came to an end in 1807, when the British attacked. They feared what might happen if the Danish fleet were to fall into Emperor Napoleon's hands. Thirty thousand soldiers were put ashore at Vedbæk, north of Copenhagen, and a mighty armada besieged the capital. From September 2 to 6, Copenhagen was bombed and burned, and the British seized the entire Danish navy and every transport ship they could find.

However, it was not just for Denmark that economic progress stalled. All of Europe suffered a stagnation that lasted until around 1830.

When Løbner returned to Copenhagen, his heyday was past, and, in this respect, he was no different than his homeland. At this point, Denmark was a half-blind geographical bagatelle located on the Øresund. The Swedish had taken Norway, and even though Frederik VII's jurisdiction still included an area extending down to Eideren, there were voices who demanded that both Slesvig and Holsten join the new German Confederation. As a result, it was in question how long Jutland would be still called a Danish peninsula.

A smile tugged at fru *Løbner's* lips and for a short moment she resembled her peculiar nickname: *Sildahøvdið*, or "Herring Head."

"Now I know you," she said, placing a hand on Old Tóvó's arm. "You're Tórálvur from Geil."

She gestured to the outer door and asked him to follow. On the other side of the walk lay the county administrator's yard, and within it was the storehouse. She kept the key to the padlock on a cord around her neck, and when she opened the door, Old Tóvó put his hand to his heart.

Oh, what a beautiful sight! Several handsome barrels of salted meat stood there on the floor. Besides whale meat and blubber, she also had lamb and guillemots in brine. On a trough sat some lightly salted mutton packed in white cloth, and the shelves held several jars in which fru Løbner had preserved berries and rhubarbs and mussels. Particularly inviting was the smell of two smoked pork sides; some smoked trout was also hanging there.

Nonetheless, the best smell of all came from the dried mutton legs. Fru Løbner inspected the shoulders and found one that was sufficiently furry. She untied he knot, wrapped the greenish shoulder in a cloth, and told him not to say another word about it. She also gave him a jar of rhubarb jam, saying that it would undoubtedly do fru Betta some good.

That evening the inhabitants of the Geil house ate barley loaves and *skerpikjøt*. But no one had much of an appetite. Martimann was unable to eat at all, only managing a couple of spoonfuls of warm milk. He had gotten so weak that Old Tóvó had to press the scraped-off mite coat against his molars, and Martimann tried his best to suck some strength from the Løbner storehouse's gift. His cough had diminished somewhat; the sound that came from his throat was more like a weak wheeze.

While Old Tóvó sat and watched over Martimann, he did as he had so often done before, he hummed his homemade rhymes. He did not know if Martimann heard him, but Little Tóvó lay perfectly still on his bunk and listened.

Grandfather sat there and rocked with his arms crossed over his chest. It was difficult for him, especially when it came to reciting the old Catholic lays against wrong deeds. However, he also sang about Grandma Pisan, and then his voice became small and faint.

———

Nå med JERN

Gudbrandsdals
OST

Amour

(short story)

NARA VARDANYAN

Nara Vardanyan has been published in Armenia since 2006 in such literary magazines as *Gretert, Garun, Inqnagit, Narcis, Granish*, and *Grakan Tert*. She was a founder of the *Gretert* youth literary periodical of the Writers Union. Since September 2012 she has been co-editor of *Gretert*. She has won several awards, including the Youth Prize of the President of Armenia for her short story collection, *Awaiting for the Independent*, in 2011. The present short story won first prize of the Guyn Literary Award in 2014.

Translated from Armenian by Nazareth Seferian.

I live on the fifth floor of one of those buildings from Khruschev's time. I go to work like regular people, come back in the evening, have dinner, rarely breakfast, and have a cat. My mother and sisters sometimes come to clean my house, so that I can write. If there is a mess around me, I don't tidy it up, but I don't write either. The messy house stops me from writing, but laziness stops me from tidying up. I have a cat because it washes and cleans itself. She's a pretty cat, with gray fur and even grayer eyes. She lies on the windowsill, under the sun. She is even prettier under the sun. I photograph her, and she closes her eyes and curls up with the click of the camera. My mother has come and removed the curtains, so that she can get them washed. She says, "Writers are lazy people, they'll sit around doing nothing all day if you let them, just thinking, thinking . . . What do they think about so much? Two plus two is four, after all." I'm standing in front of the mirror and have spotted some white hairs on my head, so I'm plucking them out. I'm plucking and at the same time saying, "Mom, what are your thoughts on sparrows, then?" and she says, "A sparrow is just a bird, nothing more," and starts to clean the windows even more fervently. The glass is so clean, that I hit my head against the window as I try to look out into the yard. I go out onto the balcony. There is a woman sitting on the balcony of the building opposite mine, also on the fifth floor. She has white hair. She is smoking. Our buildings are so close that I can see her smoke, but I can't tell whether it is a regular cigarette or a slim, and whether there is smoke, or not.

Once again, I'm living a regular life, going to work, coming back and reading a book. My mother has brought the clean curtains and hung them. I've picked green curtains this month. I have a pretty box. Inside, there are curtains selected and sewn based on my mood. Curtains are very important to me, in general. They are protective depending on their color, transparency, and the flowers or black and white spots on them. There are other things in my box as well—shawls, the socks from my childhood that my grandmother had knitted, my silver rings, and in the box there is a smaller box with a hookah. My cello is next to it. True, I never learned how to play it, but it's beautiful, so I've put it in a corner and admire it. The thin feminine neck, the brown body of a Negress, its tight strings—it's beautiful, in a word, and I like it, so I keep it. My mother sometimes roughly cleans the dust off it. I've left a spot for a lamp in the room. I've seen one and I will buy it—big and beautiful, with brown fringes.

I gather the green curtains in my hands now and look—there is a blurry light in the woman's place in the opposite building. I pull back the curtains, put my chair right up against the window and sit. Makurik purrs her way into my lap and curls up. I pat her as my fingers caress her thrumming body. She's purring, I'm thinking. They say that thinking is essential to writing, but then I'm not really thinking, I'm observing my old lady. She's coming and going slowly in her house. She has no curtains. Her windows are not that clean. The dirt has left a white film on them. Nobody else seems to be in the house. It looks like the lady lives alone. Well, solitude is a good thing. You can wake up when you want and walk around the house as you like—naked, half-naked, sitting and standing up like that. Yes, I like solitude.

I'm living a regular life again, going to work, coming and having dinner. I put the chair down, pull back the red curtain, pull myself into a corner and sit in front of the window. In the morning, granny had sat on the balcony in her nightgown. She was probably drinking coffee or tea—I say probably because the distance between our buildings is such that I can't see whether she is holding a teacup or a coffee cup.

On this occasion, I've been sitting for a long time. Waiting. She isn't there. I start to get worried. Her room fills with the light that comes from a television. My girlfriend is alive. I wonder what she's watching—a TV show, movie, cartoon, football? There are many people living in the building opposite mine. There is a newborn on the fourth floor, I saw the baby yesterday. Her mother was breastfeeding on the balcony. It's interesting, like watching people through the window of a bus. They come, go, eat, sleep, wake up, dream, sneeze, cry, laugh. The same, the very same boring and regular people.

I sit on the balcony for so long that the woman gets up, turns off the television and the house goes dark. Good night.

She was hanging her nightgown out in the morning. Her pyjamas were not shining with cleanliness. No, my mother is careful in such situations. She pours so much bleach into the laundry that the neighbors praise her, "The cleanest laundry in our yard is Ano's." She's so slow, so slow, her hands trembling—but of course I can't see that, I just feel it instinctively. While she puts one edge of the cloth on the clothesline and attaches the clip, the wind blows out the other corner and the cloth is left hanging, so she has to start all over again. You have to attach them better, woman, stronger, press down on that clip. In a word, until she manages to hang up one nightgown, I drown in sweat and, of course, end up late for work.

A new daily routine. I now only go to work like a regular person, then come back because I have an important, secret, pretty old lady. There are acacias in the space between my balcony and hers. They have blossomed into white flowers. If I could walk on air, I could step on the acacias, cross the street, step on the acacias again and end up on her balcony. That was the distance between her house and mine—acacia, street, acacia.

Yes, our new girlfriend has guests today. I set up the hookah and place it ceremoniously next to me, the cat in my lap, and began to watch proceedings in the house across the street. They're probably her grandchildren. They come out onto the balcony. The grandmother behind them, lazily, slowly. They sit. The tall one among then softly pats the granny on the head, her white, white head. I drag the strawberry-flavored hookah deep into my lungs and go happily numb. It is the woman's daughter or daughter-in-law who is hanging the laundry out to dry. Smartly, quickly, her fingers hang out four lines of clothes in just three minutes. They're the granny's clothes— her embroidered underwear, some black skirts, and a robe that looks like it belongs in a Parajanov movie. Bravo, granny. You have good taste in colors.

In the evening I rush home, holding a small television under my arm. Regular people should have a television at home and watch movies in the evening with their family or, most importantly, watch or listen to the news. Most importantly. People think that if they are unaware of what is going on in the world, then the planes will not crash without them, there won't be floods, or volcanoes erupting, and no fighting. Those news items are a tribute to their existence. My cousin was serving in the army, his mother would dutifully watch the military news. Her son was serving in one corner of the army and the television would show military exercises from the other corner, but my aunt would try to spot her son among the soldiers, stubbornly, coming closer to the television. I was at their house once, and it seemed like she had found him, she was hopping about in front of the television.

My family had seen that I had bought a television and were surprised— what do you and watching television have in common? I wait for it to grow dark and turn off the light in my room too, so that I can watch TV with my old lady. I match the flickering light and the colors with the flickering light and colors in her room. It's not this channel, not this one, not this one . . . Aha, this one matches. Bravo, granny, you're watching a cultural channel. Hey, I've seen this movie. It's Hanneke's *Amour*. We're past the halfway point in the movie. I know it by heart. This movie will kill my granny. Come on, lady. Please don't watch this. I wonder if she's watched the scene when they're having breakfast, and the woman freezes an egg for her husband. Or when the husband is afraid of his wife's blank stare. You shouldn't watch this. Turn it off, my dear, don't watch it, I beg you. I want all the electricity in the whole world to go off.

The old people have come together. The actor is eighty-five years old, the actress—eighty, the director—seventy. Over two hours, they slowly move on the other side of the screen, with infinite love for this world. Now I'm watching the scene when the husband exercises his disabled wife's dead leg. There are no shocking scenes in the movie, but the director comes and sits next to you, whispering in your ear for two hours—you have to understand that we are all going to die, death is a horrible thing, just as old age is offensive to humanity. Death is not pain, it is an insult, a boring insult. I had found myself attached to this movie so much that I had almost rearranged my furniture to match the set up in the movie—the bookshelves, guest room, kitchen, curtains, and I had ordered the same wooden chairs. The house was so beautiful—a house where the woman had died with such difficulty . . . it is difficult to die in a beautiful house.

I want the lady to stop watching the movie, to never watch it. What can I do? I can go to her house. I can pretend I have the wrong address at this late hour, or act like a beggar.

Now, Anna's husband wants to catch the pigeon that has flown into their house. His wife had also taken a similar fall in the hallway. The husband's knees tremble and hurt, he is tired and in despair. Life has stumbled into his house, he has no strength left. I wonder what my pretty old lady is thinking—she won't be able to bear it, this movie is about her too, either way you look at it. That's it. The poor thing won't make it, I have to save her. I go out, the cat still in my arms.

I wake up sadder and more tired than regular people, even the most regular of them. I went to her place in the evening, naturally. I reached her door. I heard music, the bitter humming of a cello. I knew the movie by heart, there was no such music in it, that was Schubert. I pricked my ears but the cat was not comfortable in my arms and wanted to escape. I had taken her with me to avoid being alone in the dark. But she kept spinning like a top, and purring. She scratched my arms and neck in front of her door. I patted her, but that made her crazier. She screeched, jumped out of my arms and ran away. I tried to reach after her in the dark, feeling my way along the walls. By the time I reached the entrance of the building, Makurik was gone.

I came home alone. I was a bit scared. There was no longer a light in her house. I turned on the television, the movie had ended. I barely slept. All night, I kept dreaming that someone was smothering me with a pillow. Now she's out there, sitting on the balcony, staring at a spot. She's gone back in. She's opened the windows of a room, her half-folded arms lean on the windowsill, where she stands in the middle. She breathes. The sun falls on her face, her eyes, her neck. She is wearing a white nightdress. She raises her head and, her eyes closed, breathes. She breathes. Her eyes are closed. Her eyelids are probably translucent, thin, with small veins. I can barely keep myself from taking a photograph of her like that, marvelous, so beautiful, her eyes closed, filled with sunlight. I can barely resist going over, hugging her, holding her.

A woman with rheumy eyes approaches me at the bus stop, "Young lady, I've lost the money for my medicine and can't see well. Can you give me five hundred drams so that I can buy the medicine—I won't be able to get home otherwise." This is also a kind of beggary—one cries, the other laughs, all to pluck some money off you. But I feel sorry for her and say, "Well, of course you're not going to return it, but here you go." And I take out a five hundred from my money and give it to her. "No, I'll return it to you tomorrow for sure, come here at this time, my child, thank you, bless you." She is still talking as I rush to work—yeah, right, you'll return it. I get a final warning at work, they will fire me for being late all the time. The director is polite, but strict with me. I don't want to mention that I am taking care of an old woman at home. The director gets even more annoyed at my absent-mindedness and is quiet for a while, then gives me my task for the day in a strict voice.

I notice that I keep looking out for my old lady everywhere I look. My neck is sizzling where Makurik scratched me.

My grandmother lives near my parents. I had gone to help her come over, when we were celebrating my sister's birthday last month. She had said she was ill and did not want to leave the house. "Granny, where does it hurt? Tell me, and I'll call a doctor." "My child, it doesn't hurt anywhere, but when I cough or sneeze, I end up pissing a bucketful. It's embarrassing." It's embarrassing. Hanneke says the same thing—old age is embarrassing. In my mind, I wash and give my girlfriend a bath every morning and evening, so that she doesn't smell like urine.

Nara Vardanyan

The day I saw her in the street was when I had returned early from work—I now rush home from work almost every evening. I look out the balcony, the windows were closed and nothing is going on at her place. I sit on the balcony. I want to breathe like her, but I still have time. I light a cigarette. Then I see someone with my granny's Parajanov robe walking on the sidewalk. Slowly, slowly. The white curls look like my old lady's hair. The acacias slightly obstruct my view. After a few steps, she turns and walks back. It is her. Oh God. So she takes walks in the evening. Alone. I run, rushing to go out and see her from up close. My foot lands in Makurik's water bowl and it spills, I slip and land across the length of the hallway. My knee hurts. I stand and a draft causes the door to bang shut, shattering the glass on it. The glass in the windows of my room shatter too. The smell of acacias fills the house. I carefully pick up the glass, then look outside. She is no longer there. I nail a few curtains on top of each other to the empty pane, but it is still cold. I'll go to sleep at my sisters' place. That's one of the advantages of living alone—you can spend the night wherever you want.

I haven't slept well because of the pain in my knee. I get off the bus and see the rheumy beggar. She hasn't seen me. She seems worried. I hide to watch her beg money from others for her eye medicine. Five minutes, ten minutes, she doesn't approach anyone. She drags her feet as she walks slowly one way, then the other. She takes out her watch from her pocket, looks at it, then puts it back. I had left home early today, so that I could finally get to work on time. She doesn't ask anyone for money. I decide to approach her. She spots me sooner. She approaches me excitedly, her eyes shining with dampness. She extends the money through the wrinkles in her palm, "You're here? Take this, my child. Thank you very much." I'm shocked. Every hair on my body stands in goosebumps. "There's no need for this, don't return it, my dear." I rummage through my pockets, I don't have a lot—two thousand drams, here, take it and buy medicine. She doesn't take it. She tremblingly puts the five hundred drams in my palm. I hug my little rheumy lady. I hug her tight. It's not the stench of urine, but the smell that emanates from all old people. I cry. She cries too. Because of the smell, I start to sniff as I cry. I'm a bad person, bad, my dear, I'm very bad, I'm so sorry. I feel like dying.

I sit in Saryan Park for an hour or two. I don't want to go to work. The vibration on my phone grabs my attention. It's my director. I don't answer. He stubbornly keeps calling. I switch my phone off. I have to get home, it's time for my old lady's walk.

I am seated on a bench on the sidewalk between our two buildings. She had come out at this time yesterday, she had walked along this path.

184

A group of elderly people walks by. Five or six people. They walk with difficulty. All of them. They barely raise their legs, almost not raising them at all, shuffling along as they walk. I guess the muscles start to grow weak if you don't raise your legs enough when you walk, and then they stop working. Later, you can't raise your legs any more. As soon as I reach my bench, they start to shout, push each other around and laugh loudly. One of them has a handful of half-ripe apricots and empties it in my lap. "You're young, you have teeth. Eat up," he says and quickly shuffles off to join his heavy-walking flock. "You just poured half your pension into her lap, old man, apricots are going to cost a lot this year," one of the younger old men jokes loud enough for me to hear. It is growing dark. I go home. The lady never came.

It has been three days that the lady has not appeared. She does not come out to the balcony in the morning. I wait till one in the afternoon—nothing. I go to work. There were people at her house yesterday. The light is on in the evenings. I quickly return. My sister has arrived with her children. We exchange a few rare words. The children take my box of pens and mess about with my papers. I'm irritated. My sister washes my blue carpet and keeps looking at my face, she can't stop herself. "Step away from the window, I've come to chat with you. Let's go, you'll get the chance to sit at your window again later." This irritates me. I say—step out and go home. In order to avoid offending them too much, I walk them out.

I haven't been going to work for a week. Because of my tardiness and absent-mindedness, they asked me to write a resignation letter. It came out looking like a poem. I hugged and kissed everyone, it was difficult to leave the building. I stepped into a shop on the way back, where I had once seen a pretty dress with a blend of different colors worthy of Parajanov. I bought it. It has been a week that I've sat in front of the window as I eat, read, going to the bathroom and returning quickly to sit and wait for my old lady. No sign of her for a week. Some people occasionally appear at her home and disappear. I want to go to her place, but I can't make up my mind. I feel an incomprehensible fear.

I get a call from my village. My aunt has had a stroke. They are letting all her relatives know. My cousin is crying, "I'm washing the windows and making sure the house is clean because they're saying that there is no hope. I'm crying. I'm letting everyone know because one of her eyes is open. She is waiting, but we don't know for whom. I wonder who she's waiting for? I'm letting everyone know. Let everyone come and see her, so that her second eye closes too. I can't look at my one-eyed mother."

Nara Vardanyan

I suddenly realize that my old lady must have also had a stroke. My old lady is also looking out at the world through one eye. One is closed, one is open. She is waiting too. Waiting with one eye. For me. It is difficult for me to imagine the existence of a single eyeball in that socket by itself, rolling around, searching, yearning, crying, laughing. I have to go. I dress quickly. To the lady's house. She must have had a stroke. See, that's why she can't get up, walk—and some people come and go to see her. She is waiting for me.

I go down the stairs, walk across the sidewalk, cross the street, and I don't get hit by a car, so I keep going. I pay attention to the details around me so that later, much much later, I would still recall them. A man exits from the entrance to her building, a bag of garbage in his hand. I enter the building and go up to the fifth floor. The stairs on each floor are clean. On the third floor, a girl exits an apartment with a child in her arms. Every bang makes me jump, because I have no doubts that the lady is family to me. I walk confidently. I reach her door. Ants are roaming around under her door. It was dark the last time, I had not seen much. Now I notice flowerpots next to the stairs, cactuses with white flowers. I push the door—it is open. There is no sound. I go in. My heart is racing. I don't know how many minutes I stand at the threshold. A key enters the lock of the neighbor's door and twists inside—I rush into the lady's apartment and close the door behind me.

"Anybody home?" I ask.

There is no sound. I am in the hallway. I walk forward asking, "Anyone home?" There is silence. The sounds of the world have disappeared—no cars, no children crying, no neighbor's televisions, not a single sound. I walk forward with small steps. Then I am in the middle of the room. There is no-body. This solitude is terrifying. It is the first time that I have been terrified by solitude and silence. I don't move for a few minutes, thinking that she is in the kitchen or the bathroom. One wall of her room is completely covered in framed photographs—children, churches, old people. There were also framed pictures of animals below—two of them of cats—one gray, the other a white Van cat, and the other three next to them were of dogs. "Nicely done portraits," I think. There is a box farther in the room and a brown lamp next to it. The wall opposite the one with the photographs is a big bookshelf. I approach the window. My empty house, room and balcony can be seen from here. I see that the windows have been overtaken by dirt and are covered in a white film. I turn and see a large cello, next to a small television. My knees start to buckle. She is probably in the kitchen or the bathroom. There are some dirty dishes in the kitchen sink. I slowly start to believe that she is not at home. I just need to check in the bathroom, that's all. I open the door of the bathroom. It creaks. There is a huge mirror in front of me. A face looks at me from the mirror with empty eyes, white curly hair and a plump wrinkled face. The wrinkles descend over the neck and hang near the breasts. I can't remember how long now, but she looked at me for a very long time.

I return to the room, put the chair in the middle of the room and take off my dress, the bright colors beautifully covering the chair. I pick up the cello and weakly tense the strings. I fill the consciousness of the lonely people of the world with bitter, sour and disjointed sounds.

———

Six poems

EWA CHRUSCIEL

Poet and translator Ewa Chrusciel has two books in Polish, *Furkot* and *Sopilki*, and two books in English, *Strata*, and *Contraband of Hoopoe*. As Jorie Graham reflects, "The excitement one experiences reading . . . Ewa Chrusciel's new book is hard to describe. If one made an amalgam of Darwin, early Hejinian, Byzantine art, Near Eastern books of wisdom, Ponge, Pavese, sacred Hopi and Amerindian texts, one still wouldn't be able to come up with the magical contraband this vessel is carrying. It is thrilling, wild and salvific. In poems seeking safe passage through institutions secular and transcendent . . . these urgent works explode onto the American poetic landscape. Authenticity emanates from every word, as well as originality, sassy humor and bracing images, objects, rituals, and queries from cultures in every old world trying to find right translation into this so-called new one. I would listen closely to what the ancient and near-extinct Hoopoe conveys. It really knows something crucial."

and not to spill a single grain

Your mom welcomes you
with half-empty sugar packets
in her palms. She takes them
for dollars.

They perch like fledglings;
the puffs of white grace
awaiting their take off

"Can I hold them?" you say
and she slowly deposits them
into your hands.

Each grain of sugar
carries its own trajectories
of longing

Like the centrifugal leaps
of your mom's neurons
make her grasp the inscape
of things.

One needs to be an oracle
to hear an oracle

It hides in-between the birches. It flickers. Hide and seek. How mystery winks. An apparition of deer. The candle of his tail back into dark. *The chinks in the forest.* The winks of light into zebras on the forest floor. Stripes undulate into currents. Trees smuggle the Sacred. But the souls kept skipping into leaves, bark, wrinkles, fissures, stalks, husks. The trees, the smugglers of cemeteries with rings of psalms. They compete with children on All Souls' Day. From many winged seeds the taproots hum the Book of Hours. They dart like finches. There is no way to fix them. They hide in cracks and whispers. They listen. To what is not. They are brief and violent. They unconceal. They burst forth. Theirs is unveiling. They will light the continent for me. Tigers of wrath and light. The trees are not without Kaddish. Mimosas, Pagodas, Figs and Rowans. The soul composed of very small atoms produces small dream-stations.

1974. An old man holds a votive candle at the Polish-Ukrainian border. An ancient wax figure. His skin, a yellow paraffin. He came to Poland to get the candle for his grave. The religious votives are unattainable under the regime in Ukraine. The candle, a prayer clasped in his hands. He carries the unspoken Resurrection. Kitchen and the Apocalypse. The officer pulls the candle out of his hand and tosses it into the garbage can. Darkness, his candle. The dogwoods grow in silence. Who is the burning man? How can you know a candle from a moth? What illness springs from a lost place? Trees clasp their fiery hands. I smuggle a smoke film, ghosting. I want to carry him to the Mother of Exiles. To her beacon-hand, a glowing candle. Your huddled masses yearning to breathe free. She lifts her candle beside the golden door. A polycandela. A drumming station. The intensity of the instance burns. A fire rises above his hands.

Ewa Chrusciel

Prayer on the Runway

I take snowflakes magnified by grace. I put them in the jars. Stellar den-
drites, crystal partitions, specks of sparks. They swirl in myriad wakes.
White anarchy of feathers. Species of sacred flurries. Miniature albatross-
es in disguise. The snow glistens, it is my flashlight. I cut through crowds
of foreign solitudes. I glide through space and slopes. Meandering white
brides. The frills and flounces of woods. A flock of Dominican monks on
skis. Dervishes unveiling. Snow clasps its hands in prayer. Splashing litanies
of lifts and turns. The ceremonies of *kristianias*. Plowing the fields of snow.
Pollinating snow-lilies into powder.

White ptarmigans flutter their chants of feathers. Lift off. In what image.

Prayer

The Large Blue Dress took Matisse endless versions,

repeated rubbing out

the areas of paint, etching

sinuous lines—

Until putrid matter is purity,

the sea-water interacts with oceanic crust

of scratching colors,

until the light bleeds

into blue and blue and not blue

in its infinities

On the volcanic Azorean islands,

locals make tiny flowers and nativity scenes

out of scales of fish,

their layered rings reveal their age.

Ewa Chrusciel

196   Each canvas, a scale, a scalloped rock

       unveils light years of porousness

       until blue beads form a rosary.

       Black basalt accepts drafts,

       flutings, lineations, missing

       cavities, strata, which

       in my language means

       loss.

Prayer

I leave stones of ripples
my mouth spits out oaks, *kora*, ancient rituals,
milk from St. Mary's breast, a crest of a hoopoe,
A tulip tree, yellow birch, eye-salmon rose
fiddlehead ferns, ruffed grouse, a flock of
enunciations
ingrate spoiled insulated

Now, a shower after shower
a gestu after gestu
shindig after shindig

Mouth taps iron ghosts
bark means *kora*
keeps burning till
it brains forth

Between country and country, crocuses grow.
Do not regret a crocus when woods are on fire.
The storks align themselves with the lighthouses.
Hummingbirds calculate rates of return.
Between us a *memorare* of raw sea-weed

Left
with a poem in my mouth,
a sphere a curled hedgehog
prickly calm inexhaustible

The desire for hooks in the wall

———

Seven tree poems

MANDY HAGGITH

An acclaimed poet and novelist, Mandy Haggith was born and raised in Northumberland and since 1999 has lived in a coastal wooded croft in Assynt, in the north-west highlands of Scotland. Her forest-related work has ranged from research for the Centre for International Forestry Research to helping community organizations create visions and management plans for their land. She has lobbied at the United Nations and for international environmental groups such as Greenpeace, WWF, Fern, and Taiga Rescue Network.

The A-B-Tree project from which these poems derive is a celebration of the ancient cultural connection between nature and words embodied in the Gaelic Tree Alphabet. Its inception involved eighteen public events, one for each letter, using the trees as inspiration and blending folklore and ecology.

Being Pine

being a clamber frame for a guilder rose
being a toe-hold for a rowan's pose
being a provider to cross-bills feeding
being a nest-site for sawflies breeding
being a pitch pump instead of bleeding
being slow about sex and even slower about seeding
being a sulphur-shower pollen explosion
being a site for a cone-gatherers' symposium
being a guru of yang and yin
being supple in a hurricane
being evergreen
being turpentine
being a whisperer of verse
being in harmony with burns
being a partner in tangos with gales
being a ship's mast with emerald sails
being here despite armies and pulp mills
being an allied supplier of ant hills
being moon-tuned with tidal sap
being an orgiastic wine tap
being a green thing that stands in the way
being this swaying being, being this way

hazel

a nut in my hand
a tree in my mind

in the current
a salmon waits
for hazel wisdoms
to fall

a tree made the nut
the nut will make a tree

in the woods
time bends
its arrow-shaft
loops

life to life
fungus to fungus

Hawthorn

more knobbles and angles than thorns
all the signs of suffering
chapped skin   gnarled joints
hawless twigs   contorted limbs

would you rather be edging a field of contented cows
layered and pinned but rooted in rich deep soil
or is life here worth enduring
the minch's merciless gales?

backed against the crag   braced for storms
holding to a principle that felt like freedom
in your seedling days
dying for it now

Mandy Haggith

elder

if this tree was a poem
it would be a loose
         rambling
            scrawl

wizened trunks
       branches pitted with scars
         leaves abandoned
         without qualm
         more will grow

a robin
       more familiar with the tree
         than me
           shuttles
           back and forth
           between leafy twigs
           parallel stems
           warps of a loom

remember those dishes of nectar blossoms
     bundles of berries
       such open-handed generosity
         filling the hollow
      with exuberant
    fecundity

unkempt
      dishevelled

slumped in vivacity
teeming with ease

Rowan Woman

The eagle, demon-torn, crashed to earth.
Its head buried into soil,
beak rasped through stone,
eyes and brain rooted to a tree-form.

Above ground, wood-bones branched
feather-leaved. Blood became berries
seeded with life. So, to Greeks,
the rowan was born.

Vikings went the other way: took wood
and shaped a spine, legs, arms, head,
filled out flesh with berries,
adorned the skull with leaves.

There she was, the girl. Here I am,
the woman, finally understanding why
I need to be rooted, yet always felt
I fell from the sky.

Mandy Haggith

yew

And the message of the yew tree is blackness—blackness and silence.
—SYLVIA PLATH

shade and a conversation of crows and blackbirds
funeral clothes and the hush of a sleeping baby

mouldering bones   slow exhalation of atomised souls
shadows of time   long generations past in murmurs

furrowing bark   shudder of an arrow
dusk and the passing of badgers

frozen nights creaking with ice
dark winter days to hold onto life

deep green and quiet
so many trees   so many messages

blackthorn

puckering sour
the spiny bush squats
hushed in tart stillness
smelling of the memories
bottled in the larder

she sits in the kitchen
keeping her hands moving
thumbs circling like two small animals
taking it in turns to stroke
each other's aching shoulders

she will wait all winter
as days darken and death prowls
knuckles swelling
as the bitter sloes
loosen in their jar

until one cold march morning
when her airman
lands on the prickly doormat
and the suckering stems
break into blossoms of snow

———

Mandy Haggith

A Note About the Photographs

For forty years Mark Chester has been traveling in Asia, Europe, South America, and the South Pacific, photographing what he calls cultural landscapes, that is, pictures of people, places, and things that have touched him in some emotional, intellectual, or whimsical way.

His photographs in this volume come from across Europe: (1) Belgium—shrimp fishing; (2) Ireland—man in pasture; (3) Russia—girl by fence; (4) Switzerland—two men at *boulangerie*; (5) Sweden—men with pipes in boat; (6) Switzerland—Jura automata artist; (7) Germany—accordion player; (8) Norway—cow milking; (9) Iceland—baths; (10) Germany—folk man in Schwalm Valley; (11) France—seaweed harvest; (12) Norway—goat cheese workers; (13) Norway—girlfriends; (14) Germany—Schwalmer woman on bike, and (15) Norway—Loften Island. Cover photo is of a Viking burial ground in Sweden.

A collection of enticingly paired photos spanning his career, called *Twosomes*, is available from Un-Gyve Press.

Mark Chester is currently working on a project called "Cultural Diversity in Massachusetts." The Bay State's foreign-born account for 15 percent of the total population, and Chester has been photographing naturalized citizens to Massachusetts since 2011. There are 155 countries participating in this not-for-profit project endorsed by MIRA, the Massachusetts Immigrant and Refugee Advocacy coalition. The Bay State exhibition will be traveling throughout the state of Massachusetts through 2018 at public viewing venues, such as cultural arts centers, libraries, municipal city halls, and government building lobbies.

acknowledgments

Wiesław Myśliwski's novel *A Treatise on Shelling Beans* is excerpted with permission from Archipelago Books. Author photo by Ela Lempp.

Aurélia Lassaque's poem "The King of Golden Silk" is reprinted with permission from *Solstice and Other Poems* (London: Francis Boutle, 2012).

The chapter from Māra Zālīte's novel, *Five Fingers*, appears courtesy of the translator, Margita Gailitis. Author photo by Jānis Deinats.

All poems by Ewa Chrusciel are from *Contraband of Hoopoe* (2014) courtesy of Omnidawn Publishing, except for the first poem in this selection, directly from the author. Author photo by Małgorzata Lebda.

Christine De Luca's poem "Discontinuity" is reprinted with permission from *Dat Trickster Sun* (Mariscat Press, 2014), and her other poems here are from *North End of Eden* (Edinburgh: Luath Press, 2010).

Marko Sosič's novel *Ballerina, Ballerina* is excerpted with permission by Dalkey Archive Press.

"Orpheus in the Underworld 1999 (Dead Times)" by Vincenzo Bagnoli is used courtesy of the poet and the translator, Valeria Reggi, who also provided the author photo. Author photo is by Ennio D'Altri.

Foreign rights for *The day I learned to fly*, by Stefanie Kremser, are held by Kiepenheuer and Witsch. Author photo by Albert Fortuny.

Poems by Edvīns Raups appear in *then touch me here*, © Guernica Editions and Margita Gailitis, reprinted by permission. Author photograph by Ināra Kolmane. Author photograph by Ināra Kolmane.

The photo of Jón Kalman Stefánsson is © 2012 by Einar Falur, and *The Heart of Man* is excerpted with permission from Leonhardt and Høier Literary Agency.

English version of László Sárközi's "Inner World" is © by Andrew Singer and has appeared in *Pilvax Magazine*.

World English-language rights for Jóanes Nielsen's novel *The Brahmadells: A North Atlantic Chronicle* are held by Open Letter Books. Author photo is © by Alan Brockie.

"Amour" by Nara Vardanyan appears courtesy of the author and the translator, Nazareth Seferian.

All poems by Ewa Chrusciel are from *Contraband of Hoopoe* (2014), courtesy of Omnidawn Publishing, except for the first poem in this selection, which is directly from the author.

Mandy Haggith's poems from the A-B-Tree project are printed with her permission.

All title page photos and the cover photo are courtesy of Mark Chester.